ANGEL MOUNTAIN

Evalin Meeker called herself lucky. She ran a prosperous motel, it seemed very likely that she would marry the District Attorney, Andrew Pierce — and she had Angel Mountain practically in her back yard. But when beautiful Dr. Helen Zane arrived at the motel, Andrew was attracted to her. He was also encouraged to draw up plans for the future which would take him away from the district. To Evalin, whose only dream was to raise a family in the shadow of the mountain, this was unthinkable.

WILLIAM NEUBAUER

ANGEL MOUNTAIN

Complete and Unabridged

LINFORD
Leicester

First published in the
United States of America

First Linford Edition
published 1996

British Library CIP Data

Neubauer, William
Angel Mountain.—Large print ed.—
Linford romance library
I. Title II. Series
813.54 [F]

ISBN 0-7089-7844-4

Published by
F. A. Thorpe (Publishing) Ltd.
Anstey, Leicestershire

Set by Words & Graphics Ltd.
Anstey, Leicestershire
Printed and bound in Great Britain by
T. J. Press (Padstow) Ltd., Padstow, Cornwall

This book is printed on acid-free paper

1

TOM MEEKER came in from the garage tired and greased-stained, but smiling with boyish pride. "Nothing to it," he said. "It was the fuel pump. It didn't work because the wire was loose and it wasn't getting enough juice from the battery." He paused, a stocky, round-faced man, to study Evalin behind the desk. "But what I can't understand," he added, "is how that wire got loose in the first place. You been tinkering with that motor, honey?"

"No, Dad."

"Well, somebody was. That wire's clampcd to the fuel pump by a cap nut. Those are tightened on with wrenches. How could that cap nut work loose, will you tell me that?"

Evalin decided that she'd better not. He'd roar. The next time he saw poor

1

Bert he'd give the youngster a frying. It was peculiar, she thought, how her father could be so patient with her but never with anyone else.

He sat down. He gazed about the small, paneled office as if hoping to find the answer there. The inevitable question rose to his mind as his eyes encountered the key-rack behind the desk. He asked it.

"We got any guests who think they know something about Morris Minors?"

"None that I know of. Incidentally, Dad, my cash doesn't balance. My petty cash, that is. I'm thirty cents short."

"Some kid was in, selling cookies for the school. I bought a box. They're pretty bad, but what could I do? You tell a kid to tell his teacher they shouldn't sell bad cookies, and the first thing you know you're in hot water. The Wakelys can get away with that, but not the Meekers."

"Dad!"

"Well, it's true."

"It isn't true, and you know it. And I'll tell you something else, Dad. One of these days you'll be overheard talking like that and you'll lose your contract with the Wakelys. Then what will you do?"

"Live on your earnings." He laughed at his own joke, his teeth flashing, his grayed head bobbing in the sunshine. When he could speak clearly again he asked: "Doesn't that stand to reason? Why do you think I built all these cabins? So I could live without working in my old age, that's why."

"And when I marry Andrew?"

"You won't."

"I won't?"

"Nope. You'll marry some fellow I'll pick for you myself. And this fellow won't mind a bit supporting your mother and me in our old age. We'll get the preacher to put that in the ceremony."

Atop the key-rack the small German clock chimed two. Relieved, Evalin got up from her deskchair and closed the safe and gave its combination-knob a twirl. "Cabins 5 and 9 are open, Dad. And will you try to be choosey? The last time you rented a cabin I had to spend two days cleaning it up. And a blanket was stolen, incidentally."

"Who taught you the motel business?"

"Mom."

He glowered. But she looked so much like her mother with her blue eyes dancing and her lips twitching that sentiment undercut his indignation. "Well," he conceded, "you could be right at that. Your Mom's pretty smart. She married me, didn't she? And I notice she don't approve that Andrew, neither."

"I do."

"Will you tell a father why?"

"Because I do."

"Now that's a real explanation. I thank you for that clear explanation."

Chuckling, Evalin walked to the door. She glanced out at the April day. It was a fine one still, she discovered, with clear air and a glowing turquoise sky and sunshine sparkling on clear, damp green. Beyond the escarpment of scrub-oak and brush due west, the vast panorama of mountains and forests was strikingly vivid, with sunshine and shadows quivering on the slopes, with all the trees stirring, with all the towering, snow-capped peaks flashing a clean iridescence. She understood, suddenly, why all the guests but Dr. Helen Zane had ridden off so early. She wanted to ride off, too, preferably to one of the forests. Would Andrew be interested? The goop, he'd been working too hard! Now that that murderer had been convicted, Andrew should take a vacation. He was foolish to grind and grind, because if he kept on grinding that way he'd never live to become governor of Colorado. After all, the human body could endure just so much.

"Well, Evalin?"

"Dad?"

"Uh-huh?"

"Would you be angry, Dad, if I didn't come back after my chat with Mr. Wakely? It's been a long week, Dad. I'd like to go riding for a while."

"Huh?"

"Didn't Mom tell you?"

"She didn't. What does Wakely want?"

"That plateau land we own."

"He doesn't get it. That fellow makes me mad. There ain't a gold-mine for miles around he don't own. There ain't much useful land around here he don't own. Yet he keeps on trying to get more. That fellow's the greediest man in the country."

Tom Meeker inhaled deeply. His face was beet-red now, and his indignation wasn't feigned. He stood up and flailed his hairy, grease-stained arms. "Over my dead body!" he roared. "If things keep on this way he'll be owning all of Thorpe. Then what happens to folks like us, huh?"

"Maybe he wants it for Bill."

Again, the old trick of distracting

6

him worked. He forgot the grandfather just as he'd forgotten the tinkered with Morris Minor motor. "That Bill," he grinned, "is sure a fine feller. Other day up at Camp Travis mine, I had trouble with the truck. Bill pitched in to help me just like a hired hand. You gotta like a feller such as Bill. No airs, just a nice young feller you should marry while he's still interested."

"Well, would you object if I did go riding?"

"Ask your Mom."

"She'll say it's too late!"

"Whatever she says, that's it."

"Dad!"

"Unless," he amended, "you'll go riding with Bill. I kinda owe him a favor, don't I?"

Exasperated, Evalin went upstairs to her room. She found the three gabled windows opened wide, her bed stripped, the mattress lying doubled on the floor. Elaborately casual, her mother was cleaning the bedsprings. "Two o'clock already?" she asked. She wagged her kerchiefed head. "Time's a strange thing, dear, did you know that? One hour it just races along, and it's gone before you've known you've had it. Another hour and it practically walks with a limp."

"You could've called me, Mom. I thought I was the laborer in this house."

"I thought you'd rather sit with Dr. Zane. She's feeling lonely and mopish. There's another strange thing. When *you're* sitting around with a sprained ankle no one can be jollier than a doctor. The clever jokes they can tell! The fine, stoic way they can ignore your discomfort! But if they've just *twisted* an ankle, the poor dears, they behave as though the world had come to an end."

Evalin pushed between the bed and the papered wall. She took the cloth from her mother's hand and tossed it into the pail of water. "Another thing, Mom, I did the spring cleaning last week when you and Dad were over in

Grand Junction. It was a little surprise I dreamed up for you."

"Oh?"

"Uh-huh."

The silence was intense and very long. Then, her fleshy face pink, Emma Meeker got up and trudged over to the mattress. "I did notice," she said, "that everything was incredibly clean. I felt very proud of you, really I did."

"I thought, you see, that I'd like to go riding today after I'd finished the office work. But I knew that if you got the urge to spring-clean I'd never get out, so I pitched in and got it finished. I'll be back for supper, of course."

"It's too late."

"We'll just ride," Evalin said calmly, "up to Overlook Point. Andrew needs a change. That trial wore him out. Another thing, Mom, Andrew took quite an emotional beating. He was all upset the night before he made his summing-up speech. When you love life and freedom as Andrew does — "

9

"Dear?"

Evalin's lips tightened.

Her mother's eyes twinkled.

"We're very cruel to you, aren't we?" she chaffed. "We make you work five days a week and never allow you to do what you please. And when glorious love comes along, what do we do? We disapprove, vile creatures that we are!"

Evalin leaned down and got a grip at the other end of the mattress. She helped her mother get it on the springs, then got fresh linen from the bureau in the hall and made the bed herself.

"Did it ever occur to you, Evalin, that thirty-four is rather old for you? Or that possibly Andrew isn't the man for any number of very good and logical reasons?"

"Name one!"

"His age."

"That's a matter of opinion, isn't it?"

"Then there's his ambition."

"What's so wrong with ambition?"

"Nothing, if it's normal ambition. His isn't. You saw how he treated Mr. Drake. No one could have been kinder to a man than Mr. Drake was to Andrew Pierce. But what happened? The instant Andrew saw an opportunity to become district attorney himself, he went charging around the county making all sorts of accusations against Mr. Drake."

"That was political, Mom; there was nothing personal in it."

"Did Mr. Drake tell you that — or Andrew?"

Evalin closed the three windows and dropped moodily into her wicker armchair. She crossed her legs and stared pensively at the framed photo of Andrew on her dresser. She wondered why it was that so many people were against him. Everything he owned he'd earned for himself, even his law training. And nothing had been earned easily, either. He'd actually worked, summers, as a laborer in the mines. And until he established his practise in the county he'd worked at all kinds of odd jobs, and never once had he complained or been bitter. One night, in a mood to reminisce, he actually declared: "I owe this country a lot, Ev. It gave me a chance. Do you know that's the grandest thing any country can give — a chance to make something of yourself?"

There!

That was the man they all criticized, a man who'd had to grub for everything he had but who remained eternally grateful for the chance he'd been given to grub!

Her mother laughed softly, her hands in her apron pocket, her shoulder resting against the door-jamb. "You didn't answer," she pointed out. "I like to think that's because you're too honest to tell me a lie."

"Well, of course Mr. Drake's pretty angry. I suppose he expected to be district attorney of the county for the rest of his life. He's naturally bitter because Andrew convinced everyone they needed a younger, more up-to-date district attorney. But just the same — "

"And then, you see, there's talk."

"Involving Dr. Zane?"

"And others. And the people who talk, dear, are people I've known and respected for years. So there you have the reasons your father and I hope he really isn't your glorious love."

"Gossip!"

"A bit more, we suspect."

"Just the same — "

"I can't lie to you, Evalin. I'd love to please you, but how can I tell you I approve when I don't?"

"Couldn't you try, Mom?"

"Do you think I haven't?"

"I mean really, really try? You see, Mom, I think that Andrew's bought the ring."

"I see."

The mere thought made Evalin warm. Then she grew restless. She jumped to her feet and unbuttoned her green cotton-flannel shirt. She took off her dark brown corduroy slacks and carefully hung slacks and shirt away in her wardrobe closet. "Anyway," she said, "would you be very angry if I did go riding for a while?"

The answer was long in coming. Emma Meeker had been given a jolt. Now her hands came up from her apron pockets and she folded her arms and stood with her lips pursed and her face thoughtful, staring out one of the windows. Her work dress and apron didn't flatter her. They tended to make her short, plump body seem fuller and heavier than it was. Nor did the kerchief flatter her, either. Her golden hair with its waves and curls was her strongest asset. With her hair concealed, her face, at the moment, looked severe.

"Well, no," she finally said. "I think you're foolish to want to go riding with him. But I wouldn't be angry. I imagine that at your age I did many foolish things. Shall I keep dinner for you, or what?"

"I . . . "

"Sure, dear." Her brows arched, Mrs. Meeker laughed in quick understanding. "I'll expect you when I see you. But will you promise me this? If he did buy a ring and if he does propose, will you tell him you'll think it over?"

"Mom, I'm not so desperate I'll hurry into anything!"

"Fine."

"Not, of course, that I could be blamed if I did. Imagine having to cook and keep house for just one person beside yourself!"

"Poor you."

Grinning, Mrs. Meeker picked up the pail and trudged out into the hall. She closed the door quietly behind her and Evalin, gleeful, changed her mind about wearing just any old thing for the important conference with old Silas Wakely. Since she *would* go riding with Andrew later on, she'd be smart to look very glamorous. Of course he'd bought the ring! Sue wouldn't lie; Sue wasn't the fibbing kind. And since Andrew *had* bought the ring, and since the trial was *over*, and since he *could* think about them for a change . . .

Her bright red jersey dress?

You bet!

Sure he'd seen her in it before, but he'd liked what he'd seen, hadn't he?

And her new beige coat, of course, and her new black pumps and black handbag — she'd be silly not to wear those. After all, he might take her to dinner at the hotel, and he *was* the district attorney, wasn't he, and she *did* have to dress up to his position, didn't she?

That settled, she draped her robe over her shoulders and hurried across the hall to the bathroom. She filled the tub with hot water and bathsalts suds and gingerly eased herself down. And there, in the bathtub, she day-dreamed. When they were married, they'd build a house on that plateau land Mr. Silas Wakely wanted to buy. They'd plant a lawn and gardens, and at the rear of the property they'd build a stable and a fine corral. On days off Andrew and she would pack a picnic lunch and go roaming off to the mountains. They'd track elk and deer and bears and mountain-lions, and when they were tired they'd camp beside a clear-running mountain-stream and eat their lunches and forget the world and be content with one another. And it would be the same after their children had come. They'd teach their children to ride and they'd teach them the lore of the vast outdoors, and in time their children would come to love it all as —

Flushing, she grabbed for her washrag and soap as the door opened.

Mrs. Meeker wasn't misled. "Dreaming life away is pretty silly, dear."

A sudden thought made Evalin's eyes shine. "To be realistic, Mom, this could be the happiest afternoon of my life. Isn't that interesting?"

"Or very young, depending upon the point of view. Not to digress, I wouldn't think of doing that, but your father's worried you may agree to give Mr. Wakely an option on that land."

Still full of her daydreams, Evalin laughed. "Wouldn't that be like you selling your home, Mom? Don't you be silly."

"He may be angry, you know. Mr. Wakely's used to getting what he wants. If he begins to bully you, walk out. That's what I always do with your father, you know, and it works."

"I'll tweak his big nose!"

"Be your age, dear."

"He doesn't frighten *me*, Mom. Not very much, at any rate."

Excited, her eyes sparkling, Evalin finished her bath.

2

AT twenty-one, and beautifully dressed and groomed, she made an agreeable sight to Bill Wakely. He came down the marble steps of Wakely House and eagerly gripped her hand. "Girl," he drawled, "it's about time. You don't get out enough, did you know?"

"Hi, Bill."

"Hi, Ev. Now there's a dress. The only thing prettier than that dress is the girl who's wearing it. How are your folks?"

"Fine."

"If it wasn't you," he said, "it would probably be your Ma. Now there's a very sweet lady."

"Dad thinks that, too."

He made the old move to ruffle her golden hair. But her eyes stopped him cold, and he waved his hand awkwardly and tried to pretend he didn't really own it. "Well," he muttered, "we can cover all that later. Gramps has something on his mind. Listen, you know you can trust me, don't you?"

"No."

"Will you stop teasing?"

"Is this a business deal?"

"Sure it's a business deal."

"Then I don't trust you. And anyone who trusts you and your Gramps is plain silly. How many millions does he have?"

"Four."

Evalin's jaw dropped.

Bill laughed. A tall, broad-shouldered tow-head, his eyes a warm, twinkling brown, he put his arm about her waist. "If you can't walk," he joshed, "I'll be glad to drag you along by your hair."

Evalin found her voice. "Bill, were you joking? About all that money, I mean?"

To the extent that it could, his dimpled, sun tanned face went sober. He didn't answer with words. He simply indicated the size and beauty of the property, and the property was as good an answer as any. It was a magnificent estate that Silas P. Wakely had created in the mountain wilds. At its rear, along the slopes, were virgin forests of quaking aspens and pines. Then down the estate rolled in undulant fashion to sprawl out in all directions to fill the fan-shaped plateau. No effort had been made to break all the wild land to the landscape architect's will, but for about five hundred feet in all directions subtle effects had been wrought with rocks and plantings of trees and shruberry so that where the real landscaping did begin it looked perfectly natural and right, blending beautifully with the setting and at the same time displaying the great brick mansion to advantage. The lawns were a rich, deep green, well-kept, and maintained, no doubt, at considerable expense. Here and there stood attractive groves of trees. There was a large, kidney-shaped ornamental pool from which steam curled to indicate it was fed by a hot-springs and therefore practical in a country that could stand deep in snow for months. Then, directly beyond the pool and beyond a well-maintained blue-gravel drive, was the mansion itself with its marble steps and marble columns and bay windows and gabled windows and steeply peaked gray slate roof. If the grounds themselves hadn't been answer enough to Evalin's question, the mansion would have been. It stood solid and massive against the backdrop of forests and mountains, and it was a house only a millionaire could have had built in that country, a man with several gold-mines, a man who owned practically half the village in the bowl-like valley below . . .

She said impatiently: "I shouldn't be so silly, Bill, should I? You hear the talk, you see this place year after year, and you should certainly realize that what you don't have in your own pocket Mr. Wakely has in his."

Bill scratched his left ear. "Aw," he drawled, "Gramps isn't such a tough fellow in a business deal. Anyway, he wouldn't try to outsmart you. I wouldn't let him."

"What do you earn now, Bill?"

"Four hundred a month."

"Yet you practically run the mines. If you can't look after your own interests, how could you look after mine?"

Bill grimaced.

"And another thing, Bill. You wanted college. College meant a lot to you. But what happened? Your grandfather said no. You couldn't get that much consideration from him, could you?"

"It was sensible, Ev. Take it the way he puts it. He didn't strike it rich with the help of a college education. And after he did strike it rich, who tried to get the mines away from him? Financiers with fancy educations! Only they couldn't outsmart Gramps. See? And right now, Ev, you'd be surprised how many college fellows are taking their orders from me."

"But you wanted more, you know you did."

"Ah, maybe when you're a kid you don't know what you want."

"Anyway, Bill, that's why I don't trust your Gramps. Oh, he took you in when your folks died, all right. But he could have done much more for you than he did. Since he didn't, I don't like him and I certainly don't think I should trust his sense of fair play and I won't."

The brown eyes twinkled. "See the spitfire! Say, Ev, that reminds me. Other day way up on Angel Peak, I surprised a mountain-lion. Female. And don't you ever believe they're the cowards folks say they are. This one wasn't. She was coming right at me when I dropped her, spitting and snarling all the way."

"Bill, you didn't!"

"Look, there's bounties on them."

"And everyone should be ashamed! They live in the wilds. If they do kill they kill just to eat. And I think everyone who kills anything that's minding its own business up where it belongs ought to feel ashamed."

He laughed. "Look, Ev, let's not argue. Will you tell me why we always argue?"

She didn't get the chance, then, to tell him why. The oak door of the brick mansion swung open, and it was Mrs. Coxe, the Wakely housekeeper. She was a short, round woman with red cheeks, snapping black eyes and crisply curled black hair. She was Thorpe to the bone, a woman who couldn't be over-awed by the estate because she wasn't overawed by the vast, jagged mountains that made the estate seem insignificant and impermanent.

"You youngsters can talk later," she said easily. "Right now, Evalin, Mr. Wakely's muttering in his beard."

"Hi, Mrs. Coxe. How's your husband?"

"Mending nicely, thanks. I expect he'll be ready to work in the gardens in another month."

Evalin went past her and stepped

into the large, cheerful main hall. Mr. Wakely was waiting there at the foot of the stairs, a hand resting on the newel post. He nodded shortly, his brown eyes hard under their shaggy gray brows. "You're late," he said. "Did that ridiculous car of yours break down?"

Because of Bill she refused to be cowed. "Was this an invitation, Mr. Wakely, or a command performance?"

He gestured her into the library at the left-hand end of the hall. He strode in behind her powerfully, a big, forceful man still despite his seventy-nine years. He closed the door and gestured again, this time toward a deep red-leather chair.

Evalin winced.

"Something wrong?"

"The reds clash, Mr. Wakely."

"Nonsense."

Evalin's full lips twitched. "Are you an authority on color, Mr. Wakely?"

He sat down behind a large walnut desk. His face was expressionless again, deeply wrinkled and weathered, bristly with beard and dominated by his mighty beak of nose. The wide-spaced brown eyes regarded her contemplatively, and suddenly they did something his big figure hadn't, nor his estate, nor his reputation for being the richest, most powerful man in the county. They suddenly made her feel puny and weak and surprisingly helpless.

Flushing, Evalin took the red-leather chair.

"That's better," he said. "I'll tell you something to remember, youngster. Flippancy is flippancy; it's neither a defense nor an attack nor a useful crutch. All it is at best is flippancy — and rudeness."

Evalin broke the spell of his eyes by shifting her gaze to the fireplace. "How lovely," she said. "I like those tiles, Mr. Wakely, don't you?"

He wasn't her father, who could be distracted. His bass voice demanded: "Why are you so edgy? Are you afraid of me?"

"Yes, sir."

He laughed robustly. But, significantly, he cut the laughter short. "Now look here," he said, "you have no reason to be afraid of me. I've always treated you and your folks very well."

"But not Bill."

He stared.

"He wanted college, Mr. Wakely, and you refused it. He wanted to be a farmer, but now he's a miner. If that's how you treat your own kin — "

"Your technique's amusing, youngster, but not effective. I'm curious. You attack with flippancy, and then you attack in this way. Why are you attacking?"

Evalin swallowed. She wished moodily that she were bright.

"An attack without motive," he said, "stamps you a fool."

She nodded and crossed her legs and studied the glossy black tips of her new pumps.

"Now let's stop being foolish, shall we? Care for a sherry?"

"No sir. I'm like Bill. I don't drink."

"You like him, don't you?"

"Yes, sir."

"But intend to marry Pierce?"

"Yes, sir."

"Pierce is a pipsqueak, another of those razzle-dazzle college men who aren't as intelligent as they think they are."

"And he's gentle and kind and he helps people, and he'd never never think of bullying a defenseless boy into being something he never wanted to be."

"You could marry Bill."

"I know."

"You'd be intelligent to marry Bill."

Evalin doubted that strongly. Gold was nice to have, but she'd never starve, and other things were more important. Remembering the daydream she'd dreamed in the tub, she smiled softly.

The big head with its shaggy gray chair gave another short nod. "Perhaps you're right," he conceded. "With Mrs.

Wakely and my son I was happier than I've been since. The reason I like you, I think, is that you have your feet on the ground."

Evalin was momentarily touched. And then she noticed that now his brown eyes were gleaming, and she mentally backed off warily, like an animal from a trap.

"Speaking of ground, Mr. Wakely, I thought I'd better tell you I don't intend to sell ours."

He chuckled. "Now you're using the proper technique at last. Always do that, youngster. If you'll remember always to begin by saying no, you'll discover that making money's rather easy. I thought of paying you one hundred dollars an acre. I'll now raise that figure by fifty dollars."

Evalin studied him quizzically. She wondered why he wanted the land. There was no gold to be found on it, certainly, and it was too rocky to be farmed and too far away from town to be used for business purposes.

"Well, youngster?"

"I mean it, Mr. Wakely. It isn't for sale — not to anyone. I've always thought that some day I'd want to build my home there, raise my family there. It has a lovely view, Mr. Wakely, hasn't it?"

He drummed his fingertips on the desk. "I thought, you see, that it would be useful to me should I ever decide to open up the back end of the Camp Travis property."

Its lameness puzzled Evalin, too. "How could you put a road through to your property, Mr. Wakely? You'd need a bridge to span the gorge that separates our land. Wouldn't that be dreadfully expensive?"

"Tax deductible."

"Even so — "

"Anyway, that's none of your business. I could go to two hundred, if necessary."

The idea began to appeal to Evalin. The four thousand dollars could be useful. It would make a nice sum of money to take to Andrew when she was married to him and perhaps, some day, he could help finance a state-wide campaign with it. But the trouble was that the offer was coming from Silas P. Wakely. That made it very different. If he was as rich as Bill had said he was, he'd not made all those millions by taking the short end of a business deal. There was something more involved, a something, naturally, that he wasn't telling her.

What was it?

And why was he so anxious to get that land that he'd doubled his original offer inside ten minutes?

"Well, youngster?"

She got up and buttoned her coat. "As I've said, sir, I'll want to build my home there."

"You have a better offer?"

"From whom?"

He frowned. "Oh, all right. I find the poor very interesting, youngster. No one can be more sentimental than a poor person who can't afford to be.

"Now, listen. If you do decide to sell

that land will you ask me for an offer first?"

"Certainly."

His shaggy brows arched. "Can it be," he twitted, "that you don't dislike me as much as you think?"

"Dad works for you, doesn't he? Wouldn't I be silly to antagonize Dad's boss?"

"You said that; I didn't."

She grinned, and on that odd note the discussion was ended. He rang for Mrs. Coxe, and Mrs. Coxe came in politely to show Evalin the way out. Back outdoors, however, Mrs. Coxe was an infinitely warmer personality. "Want an aspirin, Evalin?"

"Oh, it wasn't so bad. Where's Bill?"

"Changing into something decent for Sunday. He wants to take you to dinner."

"The goop! He should've asked me first. It so happens that I have a date."

The black eyes twinkled. "Oh, about that date. Andrew Pierce telephoned. It seems that Dr. Zane became worried about her ankle, and she asked Andrew to take her over to Montgomery to a specialist there. Andrew said he was sorry, but that he hoped you'd understand."

"Andrew said what?"

Mrs. Coxe shrugged. "None of my business, Evalin, but he's out with her a lot."

"Well, of course he has to be polite, and she certainly has more free time than I have, and — "

Bill came out, duded in Western slacks and a sportshirt and a jacket, his shock of tow hair plastered to his skull. He gave Mrs. Coxe a smacking kiss on the cheek. "Thanks for holding her here, Mrs. C. When I inherit all this I'll give you a raise. In fact — "

He stopped short, noticing the tense expression on Evalin's face.

He said indignantly: "I'm not *that* bad, you know."

"I — I — "

"At least I'm a loyal sort of guy. I

don't date every pretty tourist gal who comes along."

"Andrew doesn't!"

"I notice you knew who I meant!"

"You keep still!"

"What I'll never understand," said Bill, "is women. I'm loyal, I work hard, I want to make a nice home for my girl. So I get pushed 'around. But a guy like that Andrew Pierce, they all go swarming after."

Very wisely, Mrs. Coxe withdrew. In the process she gave Evalin a chance to recover.

"Say the rest," she ordered.

"And be called a liar?"

Evalin shook her lovely golden head. "No, Bill. "You couldn't lie to me if you wanted to. I know you too well. So tell me the rest, Bill, will you? I'm sick and tired of gossip that isn't gossip, of things said but not said. What have you seen, or what do you think you've seen?"

"You're too small, Ev."

"What do you mean I'm too small?"

"He wants the moon, Ev. Are you rich enough and important enough to get him where he wants to go?"

"That's ridiculous."

"The doctor is, Ev. Gramps says she is, and when it comes to money Gramps knows what he's talking about. Look, let's go for a drive."

"Bill, you don't understand!"

He sighed heavily, and as heavily said: "Maybe that's the trouble, Ev. Maybe I do."

His big hand found her arm. He gently led her down the marble steps to her Morris Minor sedan.

3

ANDREW PIERCE was startled, then disturbed. Typically, he made a lawyer's joke of it. "You're establishing a dangerous precedent," he said. "I may recall it several months from now, and then of course your position would be vulnerable."

Evalin laughed. She didn't feel much like laughing, but it seemed to her that one of those don't-give-a-darn laughs her mother sometimes used was indicated. Having finished laughing, she went back into the toolhouse at the rear of the motel property and loaded her garden cart with tools. She trundled the cart outdoors. She didn't feel much like working, either, but she knew from experience there was nothing more maddening to Andrew than the sight of her working when he wanted to talk.

"And what have I done?" he asked. He thrust his hands into the pockets of his gray flannel slacks. They were new slacks, Evalin noticed, but not a very good grade of flannel. Men, she thought, were the most impractical things ever. They never paid attention to such important items as material, color, cut or style or workmanship. So they were always stung. They had to replace their clothes sooner than they should and there went the old budget down the creek.

Not, naturally, that she cared any more. Let Dr. Helen Zane buy him his clothes. Dr. Zane was certainly rich enough, if the things Bill had had to tell her were true. What did she care how Dr. Zane spent her money? And as for Andrew . . . well, the world was filled with personable men.

"Are you afraid to talk?" Andrew asked.

Evalin trundled her cart up the asphalt service path. The path swung in a wide curve to avoid the great frame house and the drive; then it straightened out under the trees and ran due south into the parking area before the line of west-side cabins. Only two cars were parked in this area, Andrew's old Studebaker that had mountain-goat blood in its veins, and the fancy, glittering red Cadillac roadster owned by the doctor herself. Their propinquity irritated Evalin, and then she was irritated because she'd been irritated.

"Why don't you go keep Dr. Zane company, Andrew? I have so much work to do. Isn't our center lawn a mess?"

He studied the broad lawn that separated the two parking areas and lines of white-frame cabins. Here and there were scraps of paper, and some of the chairs weren't in their usual places, but those were the only flaws he could see. Otherwise it was the same tree-shaded lawn that it always was, very neat, with the flower-beds properly spaded, with the usual assortment of birds probing into the earth for the usual assortment of worms.

"Those iris are nice," he said. "And will you see your jonquils and tulips!"

"I'll be busy until dinner, Andrew. And I'm afraid this is my night to cook it."

Andrew shook his head. He had thick brown hair, nicely trimmed, and good hazel eyes under brushed brown brows. Stocky, with a fair complexion and a pleasant smile, he looked to Evalin even then like the man she wanted to marry.

She shifted her gaze to Angel Peak battering at the sky in the west. It had been up there on Sheep Meadow, she remembered, that he'd kissed her the first time. That had been a bit over two years ago, and she'd been startled, as well as pleased, because up until then she'd never imagined for an instant that Andrew had felt that way about her. It had been a thrilling moment up there all alone with just the mountains and Andrew and the sweeping blue sky. Suddenly all life had made sense, the striving and the hoping and even the dreams she'd spun until that instant when his lips, touching hers, had beautifully and wondrously brought dreams and reality together.

Andrew chuckled. As always, he had no trouble reading her face. "That girl I kissed one afternoon, Evalin, wouldn't behave as you're behaving now. That girl was honest and fair."

Evalin crossed the parking area and stepped up over the scalloped concrete trim onto the broad lawn. She picked up several scraps of paper and dropped them into one of the green trash cans. She continued on up the lawn to a chair, sat down and looked at cabin I near the creek. The doctor was still inside, she saw, no doubt lying slug-a-bed for want of something better to do. She felt scorn for the doctor. A twisted ankle was certainly nothing to complain of. The doctor should know what real hardship was. She should take a look some day at some of the miners who went deep into the shafts to do their jobs despite injuries far more painful than a twisted ankle. She supposed that she shouldn't feel scornful. She supposed that no one was perfect, herself least of all, yet the feeling grew in her rather than shrank as Andrew dragged a chair over and sat down near her.

"Andrew?"

"Yes?"

"I'm not the sophisticated type, Andrew. I should be, I guess, because I live in this time and a person should be a part of her times. But I'm not. I think of it the way my folks have it, and that's what I want, and I can't pretend I like feeling I'm just one of your mob."

Andrew whistled softly. But he wasn't disturbed. He smiled and gazed far west at the sprawling, multicolored mountains. Their lower folds were gray and purple now, and were probably cold without the warming beams of the sun. Probably within their forests animals were already busy gobbling down their last meals of the day. It would be daylight up on the peaks for several hours more, but insofar as those animals in the forests were concerned, night was already marching in.

"I don't want to quarrel, Andrew. I was hurt last Sunday because I did think we had a date. I was disappointed, too, but I won't go into that."

"I had no choice. The woman telephoned. She sounded panicky, and she's alone here, and what could I do but take her to see that specialist?"

"And that's the reason, no doubt, you've also taken her all over the county time and time again — because she's so alone here in this dreadful Wild West?"

He shot her a keen glance. "Sarcasm doesn't become you, Evalin. It makes you seem gauche, I'm afraid."

"I'm me. I won't be anyone else. And I'm sick and tired of being told how I should talk and how I should behave. Mr. Wakely on Sunday — you, now. But I notice something. I notice that neither of you cares a hoot about how you behave."

His roundish face went grim. It was his fighting face, and it was becoming well known and respected in the county, but it didn't trouble her as it had been known to trouble defense attorneys.

"I won't be bullied, either," she said sharply.

Several magpies came slowly across the escarpment of scrub-oak and brush due west. They made a pretty sight with their large black and white wings and yellow bills, and abruptly Andrew Pierce laughed.

"Now see here," he said. "I didn't come here to argue. I did what I thought I should do. I telephoned you on Monday to explain, I telephoned you on Tuesday, I telephoned you on Wednesday. On each occasion my secretary told me you refused to speak to me, and so I've come here personally to explain. What more can I do?"

Evalin rose tautly, and started back toward her garden-cart. But his hand darted out, caught her wrist. He said crisply: "Let's hear it all, Evalin."

She whirled. Her face was flushed now, her blue eyes blazing. Some of the wild seemed to be in her, yet when she spoke there was surprising calm in her voice.

"What about the drive-in waitress, Andrew? What about that redhead who works in the variety store? What about your secretary and a certain teller in the Montgomery Bank and about seven others I could name?"

He got up, his jaw thrust forward. "Is that what you think of me?"

"I asked you a question, or a series of questions."

"What have you been doing, spying on me?"

She suddenly wanted to cry. It all seemed so horrible to her. She was fighting with Andrew, the same

Andrew she'd thought would propose last Sunday.

"You don't answer, I notice. And perhaps it's best that you don't Evalin. I think you should feel ashamed."

"*I* should feel ashamed."

"A grand love, when you feel it's necessary to spy on me."

"I didn't spy. I didn't have to. Bill and — "

She gasped.

Exultantly, Andrew Pierce pounced. "Bill, eh? He's your source of information? You're amusing. Didn't it ever occur to you that Bill would like to see us split up?"

That had occured to Evalin, of course. And so she'd done a certain amount of checking. It hadn't been difficult. A girl who'd been born and raised in the valley had friends, and the friends had eyes and tongues and a willingness to talk.

"No answer?" Andrew Pierce mocked. "Well, I should think not."

"What about them, Andrew?"

He turned and went angrily toward the parking area. "I won't say any more, Evalin. I'm too disgusted to say any more. When you've apologized, we'll talk."

"What about them, Andrew?"

"And I won't be badgered into snubbing people I like, incidentally. I'm now going into cabin I to see Dr. Zane. If you don't like it that's too bad."

"If you set foot in that cabin I'll call the constable and have him put both of you out. Single women don't receive male visitors in our cabins, and you know that as well as I do."

But there was no stopping Andrew Pierce. His face was fighting mad, his strides vigorous, he went down the line to the white-frame cabin near the creek. He banged twice on the door, then pushed the door open and strode in.

Evalin inhaled deeply. She hurried back to the big house and rushed up the steps to the broad, wide porch.

Dr. Helen Zane laughed. Established

in one of the wicker armchairs, her legs resting on a cushioned wicker footrest, she had the joyous expression of a woman who saw life marching nicely to her will.

"Was it a good scrap?" she asked. "I wish I could have overheard it. You were going at one another hammer and tongs, and I don't know who looked more upset."

Discomfited, Evalin went back to the porch rail. "I didn't know you were here, Dr. Zane. Shall I telephone Andrew in your cabin? He seemed anxious to see you."

"Are you very angry with me?"

"No."

"I like this motel, Evalin. My cabin is very comfortable and the creek is company during the night. Your dinners are simply marvelous, and as for the scenery — well, I wouldn't want to leave your motel if I didn't have to."

"I don't own Andrew, Dr. Zane."

"Call me Helen."

Evalin forced a bright smile. "Oh, I wouldn't want to be that familiar. How's your ankle?"

"Very much better." Dr. Zane looked down at the taped ankle in question. "I've been concerned about it because I fractured it several years ago. There was more pain, I thought, than there should have been. I thought that possibly I had cracked one of the bones. That was why I went to Montgomery to have the ankle X-rayed."

Evalin bit her nether lip. She felt shamed by the expression on that lovely face: she wanted to cut and run for it.

"Well, no matter, Evalin. I should be myself in another week or so. Are you in love with Andrew Pierce?"

It caught Evalin off guard. Her quick flush betrayed her, and the doctor from New Jersey sighed.

"It's none of my business," Dr. Zane said, "but he does strike me as being somewhat old for you. And perhaps, shall we say, a bit too experienced?"

It was well-meant. So it didn't anger Evalin. It simply puzzled her. She sat down beside the doctor and studied the broad-browed face, the soft white skin, the mobile mouth, the chin with its fetching little dimple. She thought that Dr. Helen Zane was beautiful enough to be a motion-picture or television star. She wondered why the woman had become a doctor, since she seemed so disinterested in practising her profession. And then, automatically, she wondered why she wasn't doing her own job of gardening out there on the broad center lawn. Come next week the cabins would begin to fill up, and there'd be little time for whipping the grounds into order. There'd be guests who'd want to ride, guests who'd want to mountain-climb, guests who'd want to picnic, guests who'd want to swim, guests who'd want to pile into the motel station-wagon for sight-seeing trips through the whole darned range of the San Juan Mountains. She couldn't afford to sit there with Dr. Zane, nor could she afford to allow the Andrew business to upset her. With summer coming on the season for making money was at hand, and —

"Believe me," Dr. Zane said softly, "I didn't mean to offend. I rather like you, Evalin. You're such a sturdy, self-sufficient, unspoiled creature, truly you are. I simply thought — "

"It doesn't matter. I'm not the one and only, nor are you, Dr. Zane."

The lovely gray eyes flew wide. "I?"

Andrew came out of cabin I. What he'd been doing in there so long Evalin couldn't imagine. Probably, she hoped, he'd been sulking.

"Shall I call him, Dr. Zane?"

There was no need to. A Buick Roadmaster came rolling between the stone gateposts near the creek, and Andrew flagged it down and bummed a ride the three hundred yards up to the house.

"Business is picking up, eh?" asked Dr. Zane.

That reminded Evalin of an important business matter. "Have you decided about the summer, Dr. Zane? We have more requests for reservations than we can possibly fill."

"Oh, I'll stay, all right. Having fought through a Colorado winter, I intend to enjoy a Colorado summer. I'll give you a check this evening."

Evalin nodded, went back into the house and into the small paneled office. She was making the notation in her register when the owner of the Buick came in. She smiled mechanically.

"Good afternoon, sir. Looking for a cabin?"

He nodded. His was a tired face, the face of a man who'd been driving too many hours through the difficult passes. "Anything will do. That's a hard drive from New Mexico. I should think the state would improve the roads."

"Our population's really pretty small. And mountain roads are expensive to build and maintain. We use a lot of our tourist dollars to build and maintain roads, but there are always slides and — "

"Yes, I imagine so."

He took the proffered pen, signed his name. "I'll take a cabin for a week," he announced. "Oh, and do you rent them for the summer?"

Evalin checked through her book. "I'd have to know by the end of the week, Mr. Jackson. Actually, we don't have enough cabins to accommodate the crowds."

"Why not?"

She laughed and got the key of cabin 9 from the rack and led him toward the porch door. "The season's too short, Mr. Jackson. It would be a lot of money to keep idle during the winter, wouldn't it?"

"Well . . . "

But they'd reached the porch. Evalin smiled at Dr. Zane and Andrew made the introductions. Mr. Charles Jackson bowed, and Andrew, getting up, began to offer his hand.

Then something startling happened. "Jackson?" Andrew asked. "That name's familiar. Charles Jackson? I think — " He broke off.

Charles Jackson chuckled.

"The same, I'm afraid, Mr. District Attorney."

Andrew's hazel eyes went granite hard. "I see. Well, Jackson, I'll say to you now the same thing I wrote you: don't try any game here. I'll be on you like a ton of bricks."

"And will Wakely properly reward you, Pierce?"

Andrew spun, glared at Evalin. "If you're smart you'll check him out."

It was, thought Evalin, as good a chance as any to needle him. She laughed softly. She deliberately linked her arm around Charles Jackson.

"Don't be silly," she said. "He's too cute. Dr. Zane, isn't Mr. Jackson cute?"

Dr. Zane and Andrew were speechless. Not so Charles Jackson, a tall, slender, good-looking man with crisp black hair and sparkling blue eyes. "Ah," he said, and the south was in his tones, "I'll bet you say that to all the boys."

Together, they went down the porch steps.

4

THERE were no explanations from Charles Jackson and none from Andrew. Andrew drove off in a hurry, and after eating dinner like a starved man the handsome and mysterious Texan wearily went off to bed. In the kitchen, of course, Tom Meeker and Emma Meeker speculated. Emma Meeker said quietly, "He's probably a terrible murderer. If I wake up dead in bed, Tom, will you remember that I loved you in spite of all?"

Tom Meeker grinned. "A nice boy. You can always tell by the way a feller takes your hand."

Evalin dutifully gave him the cue he wanted. "What do you mean, Dad?"

"Well, he shakes hands the way Bill Wakely does. Like he meant it. Like he thought you're as good a man as he is. I sure do think that Bill's a pretty nice guy."

Evalin put the last of the dishes into the sink. She felt tired herself after the long day of work and tension. She wanted to go to bed. Paradoxically, she also wanted to saddle a horse and go for a moonlight tramp through the foothills. Perhaps she would. The moon would come up around nine, and it would be a full moon, and all the world would be bathed in its clean soft silver. Perhaps if she rode up to Over-look Plateau and got some fresh mountain air into her lungs, she could think. She had to think. After all, Andrew had answered none of her questions. His answer to each question had been an accusatory question designed not only to distract her but to make her ashamed of herself. She couldn't just forget the whole thing. She'd not been wrong to think her thoughts and ask her questions. She'd never once dated anyone else since that stirring night in November when he'd won the election by his smashing plurality. That was to say, until last Sunday when he'd left her all dressed up with no place to go. She'd been faithful to the dream, in short, and she'd had the right to expect him to be, and since he'd not been she'd certainly had the right to resent and to question. Perhaps the thing to do now was to see others, to show Andrew that two could play at that rotten game.

"I said," said her father, raising his voice, "that I sure do like that Bill."

"Or perhaps he's a thief?" speculated Emma Meeker, smiling.

"Who, Bill? Now there's a nasty thing to say."

"Mr. Jackson, Tom."

"Nope. He's got a good handshake."

Evalin washed the dishes quickly and rinsed them and set them in the wire-basket to drain. She stripped off her rubber gloves and grinned at the two of them sitting near the stove. "I don't think either of you is being a bit funny. Why don't you go out to the living-room and let me finish cleaning up this place in peace?"

They didn't. They never did. For as long as she could remember the kitchen had really been their living-room, with a chair for each of them near the stove and a good supply of reading material in the magazine rack her father had built himself. There, at least, they had the opportunity to get away from business, to live their own lives, to talk about the things that mattered to them. From time to time, the needs of business demanding it, one or the other would make a trip to the living-room or even out to the cabins, but always the wanderer would return to his kitchen chair to enjoy a proper family life.

Evalin took off her apron and hung it on the hook behind the cupboard door. At the mirror she patted her hair into place, then turned and with a great show of fatigue started across the large room to the hall door. "Well, I'll do the glad-handing. Only it does seem to me I do most of the work around here."

It didn't work. Her parents remained put. And since she could hardly back down, she had to continue along the hall to the large living-room up front. She found the Denbys enjoying chess and the Randalls reading and the Browers busily scribbling on postcards. Dr. Zane wasn't anywhere to be seen, which was a help, but old Mr. Linden was very much on hand and looking bored, which wasn't a help at all. She dropped lightly into a chair near his.

"Have a nice day, sir?"

"That I did. I walked. I walked along Oak Ridge Trail to the slough. Then I went down Box Canyon Way to the falls. I think I saw a bear."

"Really?"

He scratched his chin, a wizened man with a prominent Adam's apple and pop eyes. "I wasn't afraid, you understand, but I got away from there."

"I doubt they'd be this low so early in the year, Mr. Linden. There's all sorts of wonderful food for them up in the forests."

"I don't like to be called a liar."

She was patient and tactful with him. "I just thought it was possible that you'd made a mistake. See anything else?"

"I met Silas Wakely up near your meadow. I thought he might be trying to steal one of your horses."

Evalin came alert. "That's interesting. He seldom goes to the hills any more. He told someone once that he'd had enough of the hills."

"He didn't behave that way. There he was tramping around like a young feller of sixty. He was rude when I spoke to him."

"He's that way, Mr. Linden. He grew so used to being alone in the hills that — "

"It's the gold that does it. There's nothing like gold to make a fellow crabbed."

Evalin barely repressed a smile. She felt like saying there was nothing like chemicals, either, to make an old man difficult. But instead she asked:

"What did he seem to be doing, Mr. Linden?"

"He wants your property. You can always tell when a person wants something. That person has a peculiar gleam in his eyes."

Evalin nodded. "You're right, sir. He offered me two hundred an acre for it. That's a pretty good price, isn't it?"

"Don't sell, lass."

"I won't. I'll build a lovely home there some day. And my children will have the mountains as I've had them. Mr. Linden, wouldn't you like to play cribbage with my father? You could come into the kitchen, and later on Mom would make you some cocoa."

His face grew pinched with suspicion. "What do you want, lass?"

"Nothing."

"Youth isn't kind. Youth is cruel, savage. When youth is kind to the old, youth is after something."

She was almost glad, in that instant, that neither she nor her parents were rich. How horrid to have to be so suspicious of the motives of the people who were nice to you!

She stood up, smiling broadly. "You're our guest, Mr. Linden. Naturally, we want our guests to have a good time. That way, do you see, we keep our customers and our business prospers more each year."

He wasn't to be stampeded into accepting that. His bony hands folded on his lap, he pondered several minutes. But he did nod presently, and he did get up to get a good grip on her strong right arm. "Well," he said, "that does make sense. Nothing personal in my comment, you understand. A man has simply to be careful."

She thought a jolt would do him some good.

"Is that why your children and grandchildren write you so infrequently?"

"No impertinences, young lady. I shall leave!"

The other guests looked up, distracted from their activities by his very loud and angry voice. Everyone smiled, and then Mr. Denby essayed his usual role as peacemaker. "If you leave," he twitted, "your cabin will be taken up promptly. Then when you wanted to come back, Mr. Linden, Evalin here would have to refuse you."

The old man winced. He changed his mind, not without dignity. "Your food," he announced, "once again compels me to change my mind."

He went into the kitchen to play cribbage, leaving Evalin more thoughtful than ever and more anxious than ever to get outdoors alone somewhere to figure everything out. She got her plaid surcoat from her room and went out to the stables at the rear of the property. Mighty Hunter nickered and came running, but Prince, bigger and heavier and more determined, shouldered Mighty Hunter from the rail. A very wet nose nuzzled at Evalin's face. She laughed softly, then went into the stables to look for Bert. He heard her steps and whistled from the tack room. His shirt tails dangling, hay clinging to his levis, he opened the tack room door and respectfully stood aside so that she could enter. He looked just a bit annoyed with her.

"Hi," he growled. "Want something, Miss Evalin?"

"I thought I'd go riding. Care to protect me from all the savage beasts in the savage night?"

"Who does my lessons, Miss Evalin?"

"Couldn't they wait?"

"Life doesn't wait, Miss Evalin."

He went over to his desk and sat down. His hair was tousled, his thin face looked drawn and tired, and she imagined that Andrew had looked that way at Bert's age when he'd been doing more or less the same thing that Bert was attempting to do. The cost, she thought, wincing. True, they got ahead in the end; wasn't Andrew proof of that? But all the good years were thrown into that hopper of ambition, and they grew older without ever having been young.

"Bert?"

"Yes, Miss Evalin?"

"I've been doing some thinking, Bert. Surely there's an easier way for you to earn your education."

Fear, quickly erased, came to his thin, freckled face.

"I mean this, Bert. Bill Wakely would give you a job. You'd draw better wages than I pay you, and by the time you were ready for college you'd be able to concentrate on just that."

"I like it this way, Miss Evalin."

"Why?"

He was impatient with her. He clearly resented the interruption and the small-talk, but because she was his boss he swung around in his chair and said quietly: "This way, you see, I live close to town. When I'm stuck I can go to one of the high school teachers. If I worked for the Wakelys I'd live up at the mines. And I'd be too tired to study effectively, don't you think? This way, even if it does take longer, I'll learn more and I'll learn it more thoroughly."

It made sense to her, and she

shrugged. "Well, suit yourself, Bert. By the way, did Dad speak to you about my car?"

He grinned ruefully and pawed through his shock of brown hair. "I guess I'd better leave that car alone, Miss Evalin. How did he know I was the one who loosened that cap nut?"

"Dad's psychic, Bert. Either that, or he knows fellows. Well, I'm sorry you won't go riding with me. It's going to be a beautiful night."

She got up and walked slowly to the door.

Bert stopped her dead.

"What's wrong, Miss Evalin? You can tell me."

She turned, surprised. "Does it show?"

"It shows. Look, Miss Evalin, I don't poke my nose into other people's business. But you and your Ma, you've been all right to me. So will you let me say something without getting angry?"

"Such as?"

Bert's mouth went grim. "There's

much going on in this town, Miss Evalin, you don't know anything about. The Wakelys are mixed up in it; so is Andrew Pierce."

"What is it, Bert?"

"I don't know that. It has something to do with land. I heard Bill Wakely and Andrew Pierce talking about your pasture the other day, but before I heard very much they noticed me and drifted on."

"Gold?"

Bert laughed. "Wouldn't that be fine? Then you could give me the money for my education. No, it isn't gold. That land's been worked over pretty thoroughly."

"I can't imagine any other use for it."

"But what I started to say was this, Miss Evalin. You're just wasting your time on Andrew Pierce. So if he's what's wrong, I'd stop worrying about him. You should just worry about the things you can do something about. That's what I do."

"You're very bright for seventeen, Bert."

"Bright enough to know this, Miss Evalin: that Andrew Pierce would throw you aside in a minute if he thought it would help him get ahead."

"Now listen — "

"You said you wouldn't get angry!"

"I said no such thing!"

"It was implied!"

"Just the same — "

"Anyway," he broke in again, "that's what I think and I won't change it."

Evalin turned impatiently and went back into the night. Overhead, now, all the stars were blazing and the moon was brilliant over the saw-toothed rim of the Amphitheater. In the moonlight the mountains had a delicate, ethereal beauty that made her catch her breath and long more than ever for a ride to one of the forests. But it was too late for that, she decided. She'd spent too much time chatting with her folks and Mr. Linden and Bert. Talk that had come to nothing! Why did she spend so darned much time in talk, talk, talk?

Angry with herself and the world, she went up front to the center lawn and sat down in one of the chairs. She heard an owl hoot somewhere under the moon, and presently she heard another owl answer.

She wished she were an owl.

How wonderful to roam the night sky, to look down on all the wild, moonlit beauty of the eternal mountains and forests and gleaming, singing mountain streams.

How nice to be away from all this mess.

She sighed and became the manager of the Meeker Motel and Vacation Resort once again. She smiled at the tall, slender figure that had materialized from the darkness of cabin 9.

"I thought you were sleeping, Mr. Jackson."

"Strange bed and all that. Would you object to company?"

"Not a bit. But I won't stay out

very long; these nights grow cold pretty fast."

He sat down, raised his face to the starry sky. "Pretty country around here. I should think tourists would love it."

"They do."

He said casually: "Does your district attorney work for Silas Wakely?"

Evalin went tense. "That's a strange remark, Mr. Jackson."

"I could make a stranger one."

"Well?"

"I'll offer you double the amount Silas Wakely offered for your land, Miss Meeker. What do you say to that?"

She said nothing.

She was too dumbfounded and startled to speak.

"You see?" he laughed. "Don't ever challenge me again."

5

ELIBERATELY, Charles Jackson of San Antonio, Texas, dropped the matter there. He returned to cabin 9, where he had a good sleep, and the next morning, early, he dressed in sports clothes that could take rough treatment and drove down into Thorpe for breakfast. At that hour the small village reminded him of ghost towns he'd seen all over the West. No smoke curled up toward the shadowed sky, nothing moved or barked, no light was to be seen anywhere. There were the mountains hemming it in on all sides, there were the forests spilling down as though to inundate the half-dozen streets and some fifty houses in tidal waves of botany. But this very deadness appealed to Charles Jackson. Such villages, when they were surrounded by such spectacular scenery, were very popular with tourists who yenned for a real taste of the Wild West. He must remember, he thought, to get a photographer to snap pictures of the town before any changes were made. Properly used to illustrate properly written advertising copy, the pictures would quicken interest in Thorpe and help him and the Syndicate to make a nice return on their investment.

He swung left off Cougar Way, which appeared to be the village's main street. He spotted a gasoline filling station two blocks south and, turning left again, saw the towering pine indicated on his map. There, he was relieved to see, stood a house with lights in the windows and smoke curling up from the chimney. He grinned. He made a mental note to increase his scout's salary to ten thousand dollars a year. The information gathered by the scout had been detailed and very accurate. Men who saw so much and who were careful to record it all were useful to have on the payroll. And as the Syndicate expanded such men would actually make excellent regional managers.

Charles got out of the car before the house and opened the gate and strode, whistling, up the path. He was instantly challenged by a dog. He laughed and whistled softly, and the barks stopped and the dog began to wag its shaggy tail. Charles gave its ear a scratch and its side a little wallop, then continued up the steps to the porch. He didn't have to ring the bell. The door was opened by an amply-curved redhead with green and amiable eyes. There was no shyness in her greeting, but no forwardness in it, either. "Hi," she said. "Aren't you up pretty early, mister — "

"Lenore Dalton, I think?"

"The same. I haven't got any chow ready, but if you want coffee you're welcome to a cup."

"Coffee will do."

Charles went into the hall and looked about, his eyes not missing a thing, nor his nostrils. He disliked the musty smell of damp, but he liked the good strong aroma of the coffee. He went into the dining-room she'd indicated and took one of the wooden chairs at the window table and gazed back to the street. He thought the park across the way looked grubby, but he rather liked the quaint brick building that apparently served the area as a kind of catch-all administration building. When the girl returned he gestured at the building. "That the County Hall?"

"Montgomery will sue you."

"I've been sued before. An employee of mine, a fellow called Vance, tells me you have information I might find useful."

The girl poured the coffee. When she was finished she carried the pot back into the kitchen. She was gone several minutes, then returned with sugar and cream. "Listen," she said, "I told Mr. Vance that I like living in Thorpe and that I'm not getting into trouble with the Wakelys."

"Fair enough."

"What did you say your name is?"

"I didn't."

"Sociable, aren't you?"

He stretched his foot out under the small, white-clothed table and gave the chair opposite an outward shove. "Sit down, Lenore. I'm Charles Jackson of San Antonio, Texas. I intend to build a tourist hotel here. I intend to do more. I intend to take about half the eastern slope of Two Peaks Mountain and create there the kind of vacation resort no one in this part of Colorado has ever dreamed of creating. Is that frankness enough?"

Her eyes rolled. She giggled nervously, but sat down.

"The information I want," Charles said, "involves the district attorney, Andrew Pierce. He flirts. Among other things, with you. So you know him, and you need money, and I have money to pay for the things that you know."

"My," she twitted, "when you do

start you lay it on the line."

"I earn a hundred thousand a year clear, Lenore. As you can see, my time's too valuable to be wasted."

A great wistfulness came into her big green eyes.

Charles understood that wistfulness for a part of his hundred thousand dollars. He'd seen that wistfulness before, all over the United States, down in South America, across the Pacific in Hawaii and even as far south as Australia. He took his wallet out and laid a twenty-dollar bill on the tablecloth.

"It spends," he drawled. "And the nice thing about that bill is there's more where it came from."

She leaned forward intently. "Just for the fun of it, let's see."

His black brows quirked. "Do you have a tongue, Lenore?"

She showed him her tongue. It was very pink and dainty.

He added a second twenty. He then returned the wallet to his pocket.

The terms settled, Charles rested his arm on the table and eyed her sharply. "Now earn them, Lenore. No evasions, please. And listen: if you're making a play for the district attorney I don't care. I'm not after anything like that. Understand?"

"For a young, handsome fellow you're awfully abrupt."

"So I've been told."

"You have to understand all this is a great surprise to me. I'd have to think. I mean, maybe I should get at least a hundred, I don't know."

What happened then both startled and pained Lenore Dalton. The money was snatched up, and in almost the same moment Charles Jackson was on his feet and striding toward the door.

"Mister," she begged, "do you have to be abrupt?"

"I'll get the information elsewhere."

"Do you have a kid?"

"No."

"Well, I do. And my husband hit for California, and if you think it's easy for a girl to earn money in a village like this to take care of her kid real fine, you're crazy. And I don't owe you anything. You came to me. It's crazy business, see? I have something you want, you have something I want, and why shouldn't I get all that I can?"

Charles was profoundly touched. That exasperated him, because sentiment had no place in business, and who knew that better than he did? Still, he thought, how could you blame a mother for battling as hard as she could for her child?

"I'm weeping, Lenore. Now tell me this place is mortgaged up to the hilt."

"It is."

"And the rest of it?" he laughed. "No shoes for your youngster and you really need medical attention and — "

He never got farther.

A great cry of fury came from her throat, and then her face crumpled and tears came from her eyes and she was sobbing hotly: "You shouldn't make fun." Taut, feeling cold, Charles returned to the dining-room and his chair. He didn't like himself at the moment. That would pass, he knew, because he was a pretty fine fellow, but at the moment he didn't like himself at all.

"You can drop dead!" Lenore Dalton said. "You can just go and drop dead!"

Charles did know enough to keep quiet. And since he never wasted time he used the next five minutes to sip the coffee. He approved the coffee. It had strength and body to it; there was none of that nonsense involving more water and more profit for less coffee.

The redhead sniffed. With dignity she stood up and said: "I will just ask you to excuse me, Mr. Jackson. I don't know anything that will help you. And whatever you're up to, I hope that you'll fail."

"Did Wakely make Pierce the district attorney?"

She went back toward the kitchen.

"Does Pierce do Wakely's dirty work?"

She reached the kitchen door.

"And is it true that Miss Meeker is a sure bet to marry Pierce?"

Lenore Dalton whirled. "That liar? I should say not!"

"How do you know?"

"Listen, the things I could tell that kid — "

"Will you?"

"No."

"For a hundred dollars?"

"No."

"For two hundred dollars?"

"No."

"Why not? You said you need money. According to you, you're desperately poor."

"It so happens there are things you don't do for money."

"For five hundred dollars?"

The green eyes bulged. "Say, you can sure throw figures around."

"Well?"

"No."

"Why not?"

"You know the sort that Meeker kid is? She sends me customers, don't take a commission. The kid was sick, my kid, that is, so I had to close up, I thought. Only the Meeker kid came here every day for a week to run this place for me — no charge."

Charles surprised her. "Yes," he said, "I know. Vance gave me that information, too. Apparently Vance is very good at his work. He said you're loyal, and obviously you are. Fair enough. My real proposition is this: I want everything I can get on Pierce. I want everything I can get on Wakely. In a place like this you hear things, and you'll hear a lot about me and my plans. I'll want that. You'll get fifty a week. When the hotel is opened you'll have a job. If it isn't opened I'll give you a two hundred dollar bonus. Yes?"

She considered this, lifting an apron corner to her face and wiping the tears from her eyes.

"Mister?"

"Well?"

"This is none of my business. But aren't you going awfully high just for info? I mean, a hotel is just a hotel. What can you make with just a hotel in a town like this?"

"I should imagine," said Charles, "at least a hundred thousand a year."

"You're crazy!"

"I'm always called crazy until I've banked the money, Lenore. Well, your answer, please."

She spread her hands eloquently. "I'd be crazy to say no, wouldn't I?"

Charles handed her fifty dollars and began to like himself again. He ordered breakfast, and while he ate he questioned her and had much of his scout's information confirmed. Thorpe was indeed dominated by Wakely, and while the county was less dominated by him, he'd nevertheless been strong enough to have Pierce nominated for and then elected to the important post of district attorney. He learned more. He learned that while a great many people were opposed to Wakely, they got their living from his mines and other interests and that in a test of strength Wakely, in Lenore's opinion, would win easily. He glanced at his wristwatch and did some thinking, then pushed back his chair. He smiled at the redhead. "Well, that will be enough for now. I'll need some more fill-in information, and of course if you hear anything interesting I'll want it promptly. I'll get in touch with you. I may eat breakfast here each day, I don't know. But . . . "

He broke off, frowning, as the door opened. His frown deepened when Andrew Pierce came into the small dining-room from the hall. But he changed his mind about leaving, because he had a strong conviction that here was the fellow who'd do most of the open fighting against him, and he wanted to size Andrew Pierce up for himself.

"More coffee," he told Lenore. Noticing she was tense, he laughed.

"Now don't tell me," he chaffed, "that you're so guilty of something the mere sight of a district attorney frightens you. I'll tell you a secret. Most district attorneys aren't as formidable as they like to think they are."

Andrew Pierce's face went grim. "Just try your games here, Jackson."

"I shall."

Their eyes locked.

As Lenore left hurriedly, Andrew Pierce strode over to Charles Jackson's table and sat down.

He said briskly: "Now let's talk this over man to man, Jackson. We like Thorpe as it is. The mines are worked all the year around. We have no unemployment to speak of. Our merchants are prosperous and life here is very simple and very good. We have the right, I believe, to keep it that way."

Charles countered quietly: "The general wages in this area are low, your merchants barely make a living, and for many people here life, while it may be simple, isn't good. And since this is America, I have the right to open a business wherever I wish."

"That's it?"

"That's it."

"Over in Montgomery they're interested in developing a tourist trade. Their Chamber of Commerce would greet you with open arms. You'd probably obtain land on very favorable terms, and probably the merchants there would make good concessions for you."

"I know," Charles said dryly. "I've received their offer."

"Well, then, why don't you be sensible?"

"Montgomery lacks the scenery of Thorpe. It's too big, for another thing. There are too many businesses. I find from experience that a proper vacation resort is one that exists in an area practically removed from the fuss and bother of business and manufacturing establishments."

Andrew's voice went hard. "Well,

we'll block you here."

"That's Wakely's decision?"

Andrew smiled. "Now you wouldn't expect me to admit, would you, that the district attorney is here doing Mr. Wakely's bidding?"

"No, I wouldn't expect you to admit that so early in the game."

Andrew stiffened.

Charles, rising, just laughed. "Listen Pierce," he said. "I've met your sort before. You're long on ambition, short on money and ability. You dream the dream many fellows in your position dream: that if you sell out, that if you do a great man's dirty work, he'll reward you by plunking you down in a governor's chair. Well, fellow, dream on. I'm willing to be reasonable, to work with Wakely in all possible ways. But, of course, I don't intend to be defeated here without a scrap. Tell him that, will you?"

Andrew said nothing. His hazel eyes were flashing with naked fury . . .

6

TO Evalin's surprise Andrew telephoned, suddenly, toward the end of the first week of May. It was a gray morning, with great gloomy clouds swirling about the mountain peaks and a feel of rain in the air. None of the guests had wandered off for fear they'd be caught in a sudden mountain storm. They'd assembled on the big, broad porch of the Meeker's white-frame house, and for want of something better to do they'd been discussing the startling announcement that had been made by Charles Jackson through the medium of the *Thorpe Golden Bullet*. "Well, I always wondered," Mr. Denby had been saying, "why some outfit with a lot of money hadn't built a resort out here." At that moment Evalin's mother had come outdoors to say: "Call for you, dear. Andrew of all people."

A nervous Andrew, Evalin was pleased to discover, an articulate man who was at a loss for words for once.

"How are you, Evalin?"

"Fine."

"That's fine."

A long silence. Then:

"I've been thinking about you, Evalin."

"You have?"

"Yes, Evalin, I have."

"That's fine."

"Thank you, Evalin."

A long silence. Then:

"About that little misunderstanding we had, Evalin."

"Is that what you call it?"

"Evalin, let's not quarrel again. I feel miserable. I think we're too inclined to be short with one another. We seem to forget that in any human relationship there should be adult give and take."

"Who does the giving, Andrew?"

"I do admit, Evalin, that I've

been seeing something of Helen Zane. Frankly, you're so tied up there at the motel that I grow lonely and — "

"Let's get married, Andrew. Then I'll be with you all the time and you won't be so lonely."

"You know that's impractical."

"Why?"

"Evalin, don't you see that I've just gotten my foot on the first rung of the ladder? A man like me has to concentrate on his career. What does this job amount to? A few years from now I may be defeated as crushingly as I defeated Drake. Then what? There's no money in a small law practise in an area like this."

"You could help me run the motel."

"Evalin, will you be serious?"

It suddenly occurred to her that he wasn't. He wanted marriage, she was sure, quite as much as she did. But the difference was that he wasn't as sure of the name of the person he wanted as she was. And so in the relationship, she was shocked to realize, he really wasn't as serious as she was, or as he pretended to be.

Her chin wobbled.

She heard herself say: "Well, perhaps you need a rich woman like Dr. Zane, Andrew. Then you could afford marriage and a political career, couldn't you?"

"There we go, quarreling again."

"You said we'd be married the day after you were elected. You said that!"

"Listen — "

"That was more than six months ago! But what's happened? I see less of you now than Dr. Zane does, yet you have the nerve to suggest I'm being unreasonable."

"Will you please listen, Evalin?"

"But I do want to apologize for one thing, Andrew."

"Evalin, I don't ask for an apology."

"I do want to apologize for having accused you of dating that redhead who works in the variety store. The redhead I really meant was Lenore Dalton. You should be ashamed. She has problems enough."

"Evalin, I'm just asking you to listen."

Evalin's temper exploded. She thought of all the dates she'd not had with Andrew, of all the fibs he'd told, of that ring he'd bought but not offered, and she threw her head back and stormed:

"I won't listen any more. When you're ready to stop playing, Mr. Pierce, come visit me. In the meantime, go ahead and do your flirting like a kid who's just discovered women."

She whammed the handset to the standard. She slumped back in her desk-chair and fought to quiet her trembling hand. The nerve of him! Did he think she was stupid? Did he think that she'd not read the *Bullet*, or that she'd been unable to figure out the reason he'd romped all over Charles Jackson the day the Texan had arrived? And did he really believe she was so stupid that she'd been unable to figure out the reason for his sudden telephone call?

She marched out hotly to the kitchen. She found her mother all mixed up in the happy business of baking several pies, and angry though she was, she sniffed at the air appreciatively. "Nice, Mom. Let's have Bill to dinner, shall we?"

"Certainly. Did Andrew want anything important?"

"Doesn't he always?"

Her bitterness surprised Mrs. Meeker. It was unlike Evalin to be bitter. Usually the girl took life as she found it, as a sensible girl should. Emma Meeker appraised her tense, angry face without seeming to, and shook her golden-gray-streaked head.

"That isn't very nice," she reproved. "Now I'm sure you know I wouldn't approve a marriage to Andrew Pierce. So I'm sure you'll understand that when I say fair is fair I'm not in effect trying to patch things up for Andrew. But the truth is you're not really being fair with him. A man like Andrew — well, a man in his position does have to get around. That's part of his job. And when you're not available he has to get around with someone else. A single man, dear, is difficult to fit into a party, you should realize that."

"But see how quickly things change, Mom! Along comes Charles Jackson with his big plans, and because I control the land Charles Jackson will need, Andrew suddenly remembers I exist. It makes me so angry I'd like to pull his nose!"

Emma Meeker chuckled. "Speaking of which, did you tweak Mr. Wakely's nose that Sunday?"

"In effect I did. Notice he didn't get the land, please."

There was an interruption. A knock sounded on the back door, and it was Helen Zane, her ankle all right now because she didn't even limp as she came inside. She made a fetching sight in green corduroy slacks and a yellow flannel shirt. Her gray eyes were sparkling, her mobile mouth was twitching with a broad, happy smile. "My favorite ladies," she said. "Evalin, let's go riding."

"Sure."

It was too complex for Emma Meeker. Baffled, she eyed her daughter's face, trying to discover the reason for that switch. She couldn't help asking: "Are you feeling all right, dear?"

Evalin snickered. "Dr. Zane," she said quietly, "is one of our prize guests. She's staying the full season, no less. Who am I to say no to a prize guest?"

She hurried outdoors ahead of the doctor and led the way across the broad back lawn to the stables and corral at the rear. Bert, apparently, had been ordered to saddle up two horses, because there Mighty Hunter and Prince stood, restless to head for the hills. Both horses were moving forward quickly and eagerly the instant Evalin and Dr. Zane had hit the saddles. Once beyond the sprawling motel grounds, the horses broke into trots, striking across the escarpment of scrub-oak and brush as though they knew precisely where they wanted to go, and why.

The gray sky and swirling clouds nothwithstanding, it was a beautiful morning for a ride. The air was cool enough to invigorate the horses, and because of the damp there was little dust to speak of. Down from the mountains, on a breeze, came deep, wondrously rich smells: pines and spruce were pungent in the air, and sweet meadow grass, and musky humus, and creeks running icy and pure with melting snow. Their heads outflung, their great nostrils flaring, the horses inhaled deeply of those smells, and Evalin did, too. She brushed thoughts of Andrew from her mind. Such small, small thoughts they were here in this eternal, magnificent immensity!

As though she'd sensed Evalin's emotion, Helen Zane smiled. "It's

96

very beautiful here, isn't it? You know, Evalin, I think I envy you. This is your home. You've had it all your life, and it's made you the person you are, and no matter where you go or what you do in the future you'll have all this with you. Yes, I'm sure I envy you."

"Why don't you practise out here, Dr. Zane?"

The woman shrugged.

"We could use good doctors out here," Evalin went on deliberately. "Of course, you wouldn't make the money here that you make in the east. But out here money isn't as necessary. You see how simply almost everyone lives."

"Perhaps I don't care for simplicity."

"What do you care for, Dr. Zane?"

"Truth. The right. Normality. And probably for my vest-pocket estate in the lovely Oranges of New Jersey, and all the excitement of the social life that goes with it. And I doubtless should say, Evalin, that I care very much for Andrew Pierce, too."

"I know."

"I know you know. I think I should also say that I am scarcely proud of myself, Evalin. I thought several times of leaving. Once I had actually made the arrangements necessary. I — you're very nice, Evalin. In your position, I think, I would have told me to leave."

"As I told you once, Dr. Zane, I don't own Andrew. I doubt anyone does, or will. Andrew was too much on his own. He's like — well, some of those old prospectors you see when you wander about the loneliest corners of these mountains. They've been alone so long, so utterly dependent upon themselves, so used to struggle without help, that in many ways they're like the wild creatures they hear and see every day. Andrew — well, he has that same wild self-sufficiency, and I think that like them he'll retain his independence to the last. Am I being clear?"

"Clear enough. I hope you don't hate me, Evalin."

"I never hate anyone, Dr. Zane.

Hate's negative. I dislike negatives."

"But you don't like me, is that it?"

Evalin met the lovely, warm gray eyes. She felt embarrassed for Dr. Zane because she intuitively knew that Dr. Zane had a great psychological need for being liked. She'd met such people before. A motel was a good place to meet them, because for some unexplainable reason such people were always on the go, spending a week here, a month there, talking and smiling, getting acquainted with others, but never really becoming a part of life anywhere.

"I think I do, Dr. Zane," she said gently. "I suppose I shouldn't, inasmuch as we're probably rivals. But as Mom is fond of saying, fair has to be fair. If I had rights it might be different. But as things stand . . . "

"You could be wrong about him, you know. Oh, this probably is what you expect me to say, but he's so much older than you and — "

"It's what I expect you to say."

The lovely doctor frowned and lapsed into silence. The horses pushed on, following the ore-trucks road now, past Lost River Gorge, into the trail that led up in a winding fashion to Overlook Plateau. Seen from that height, the village looked small and disturbingly insignificant. Evalin had to chuckle. "Not much, is it, Dr. Zane?"

"How did Mr. Wakely ever find this place, that's what I want to know."

"As much by accident as anything else. You know how those prospectors are. They're always pushing on, hoping for a big strike. Well, one day old Mr. Wakely, very young and adventuresome then, looked due west and saw the opening of what we now call Corkscrew Pass. It wasn't on his map and he thought that since it wasn't, he had a chance to explore unknown territory. He did. He was here in this valley for a year and he panned enough gold for expenses, but nothing more. And then one day he pushed on up Wakely Mountain and he struck it rich."

"And owns most of the valley?"

Evalin shrugged. "Most of the land surrounding the valley, but not the valley itself. You see, too many people came in before he could grab the valley. I imagine he's very sorry about that now."

"Why doesn't he want that hotel Jackson's talking about to be built here?"

"Probably because he won't control the village in the valley as he has for the past thirty years. In a country like this control can be pretty important. If there's no other source of income, the man who can offer you a job has things nicely his own way. That may be hard on the people, but it isn't hard on him."

Dr. Zane nodded her glossy black head. "I can see that, of course. Still, the sensible thing for him to do, it seems to me, is to come to terms with Charles Jackson."

"Silas P. Wakely?"

Dr. Zane whistled. "It's that bad?"

"Oh, he's kind enough and fair enough, I suppose. But the idea of him, the pioneer, sharing power with a Johnny-come-lately — well, he isn't that type."

"Can he freeze Jackson out?"

"He can try."

"With the help of Andrew Pierce?"

Evalin gave her a long glance. "Andrew has ambition, Dr. Zane. He'd like to be governor. Who knows what an ambitious man will do if he's promised support?"

"Would it be illegal to prevent Jackson from locating here?"

"I don't think so."

"So that if Andrew Pierce, as an ordinary citizen, say, did help to prevent him from locating here, he wouldn't be doing anything wrong?"

It was a tricky thing, Evalin thought. And Dr. Helen Zane was missing the point. The point wasn't the legality of the question. The point was that a hotel such as Charles Jackson wanted to build, and a tourist resort such as he wanted to create, would be a wonderful thing for the valley. As things stood now the prosperity of Thorpe was too dependent upon the prosperity of the Wakely enterprise. Should any of the veins peter out the people of Thorpe would be that much poorer. Should the government lower its price per ounce the people of Thorpe would be less secure. That was bad. Any town that was so dependent upon one industry or enterprise was a town built upon quicksand. In order to endure, a town needed as much industry as it could get. And there, she thought, was one of the reasons Mr. Wakely would find himself in the battle of his life. Strong though he was, he wasn't so strong he could frighten the people into remaining content with insecurity. People with children and homes wanted and needed security, and if they believed for an instant that the hotel and vacation resort would bring fresh money in, create more jobs, they'd do a great deal of thinking before they supported Mr. Wakely.

"You haven't answered," Dr. Zane said.

"How can I answer? I don't know that Andrew will be acting as an ordinary citizen. I do know this, though. Mr. Drake was defeated because he was accused of being Mr. Wakely's man. If Andrew becomes too involved in this he'll be endangering his career, which seems to mean so much to him."

"Still . . ."

Evalin laughed. "Ah, let's drop it. Let's have a gallop, shall we?"

Dr. Zane considered, then nodded.

Evalin used her spurs, and with Mighty Hunter in the lead the horses leaped ahead.

7

IN town a few days later to pick up supplies at the Gifford Grocery Store, Evalin had the opportunity to learn just how much security did mean to at least some of the people of Thorpe. Several men were sitting in their wooden chairs around the pot-bellied stove at the rear. They were chewing tobacco, and one was whittling, and they were talking, as people will, about this new excitement that had come to town. One man said: "I like the cut of this Jackson." Another man said: "I like the look of any feller who maybe will give me a job." A third said, "With the tourists flocking in Wakely will sure have to raise wages if he wants to keep his hired hands."

At this point Evalin was noticed and conversation stopped.

Mr. Gifford got up from one of the

wooden chairs and ambled over. He was a small man in his middle fifties, with a gray and balding head, old-fashioned spectacles and kindly gray eyes. He was neat in a black apron and new black shoes that squeaked.

"Well, Evalin," he smiled, "it's nice to see you. I don't get to see you often these days."

"Business, Mr. Gifford. Every cabin is rented and the season seems under way."

He rubbed his hands briskly. "Guess you'll be giving me a real order, eh? Will you be serving just dinners again this year? Lots of folks wish you'd serve meals all day long."

"Then I'd never get outdoors, would I?"

"Think of the money you'd make."

"Think of the beautiful mountains I'd never roam!"

"I should think," he teased, "that you'd be tired of mountains by now. You've been roaming them since you was a pup."

Evalin shook her golden head. She said firmly: "If I roam them for a lifetime that still won't be enough. And if you're going to tease me, Mr. Gifford, I'll take my trade elsewhere."

"Where?"

"Montgomery."

"That's too far and you know it."

A fellow at the rear cleared his throat. "An' don't you know, girl, that Mr. Silas P. Wakely wouldn't like that?"

Instantly, there was tension.

Mr. Gifford snapped: "No talk like that here. I won't take no talk like that here."

The tension was increased because the door swung open and Bill Wakely strode in. The big towhead saw Evalin and smiled. But he pushed on between the two center counters toward the store at the rear. His brown eyes appraised the loafing men. "Any hands looking for work?" he asked.

"For how much?"

"The usual. I need two men for the

summer. Anyone needs an advance, that can be arranged."

No one moved, no one spoke.

Bill was puzzled. "Something wrong with me, fellers? Do I smell like a pole-cat? Somebody have a beef?"

The short man who'd asked the question asked another. "Couldn't you go higher, Bill? Short-term work should get a feller maybe two dollars a day more. Stands to reason."

"Look, I don't set the rates, you all know that."

"Well," said the short man, "I can wait a while. Nothing wrong, as I see it, in a feller trying to get the best wages he can for himself."

Bill stared, arms akimbo, his weathered, ruggedly handsome face lively with surprise.

"Who'll pay you more?" he challenged. "Show me one mine anywhere in this country that will pay you more."

The short man said nothing.

Bill's hand came down to slap his trouser leg. "No one is begging, of course. It's certainly a free country, and anyone who tries to make it any different will have to battle with me. Well, what about you others?"

No one else said anything, either. They had the set expressions of men who'd decided upon a course of action and who were determined to follow it through.

Bill nodded. "As you like. Sorry to have bothered you men. I won't again."

He came back to Evalin, flushed with anger, but still smiling after a fashion. "I have the truck outside. If you'd like a short drive we could come back and pick your stuff up."

Evalin began to nod, then grew acutely aware of the fact that all eyes were boring at her face hard. It was then that she grew uneasy, for none of those eyes staring from the end of the grocery store were the friendly eyes she had known for years. Remembering some of the thoughts she'd thought up on the plateau with Dr. Zane, she grimaced. It had begun already, then, the choosing up of sides, the preliminary movements of people coming into conflict?

She looked back at Bill. "It would have to be a short ride, of course. With all the cabins filled, Mom will need me pretty quick."

She gave Mr. Gifford her list, then in a dead silence preceded Bill to the street. She got into the cab of his pickup truck and settled back comfortably as he drove east to his grandfather's headquarters over near Thorpe River.

"Nice day?" Bill asked.

"Nice day, Bill."

"That was strange back in the store, wasn't it? I mean, we've had no complaints about wages before."

"Would it have done them any good to complain? Your Gramps would have told them to quit and then where would they have been?"

"They're silly, Ev. Now you know me; I like good wages as well as the next feller. But you have to be reasonable about things like that. Gramps doesn't keep much of all that gold he mines. Take expenses and taxes, the low quota of gold we're allowed to mine — well, it doesn't add up to a fortune. Sure, Gramps has a fortune. But most of that was made before the big depression of the thirties. Nowadays . . . "

"Well, we won't settle it, will we?"

He turned the truck into the big headquarters' yard. He parked at the rear and took her hand and led her down the rolling slope to a bench overlooking the Thorpe River. The river was frothing along between its harsh, stony banks, and there were waterousels darting in and out of it with pretty flits of their wings. Across the river a chipmunk was grubbing for food in among a small grove of aspens. And farther back in the groves a mule deer was eating as though it were far, far removed from the haunts of man.

Bill smiled as they sat down. "Like old times, Ev, remember?"

Evalin did remember, and they were

good memories that made her think that most of the pleasant moments of her life had been spent with Bill. For some reason they'd hit it off practically from the moment they'd met. He'd been the boy who'd carried her books, and she'd been the girl who'd knitted him the traditional pairs of Christmas socks. They'd learned to skate together and to ride together, and despite the fact that her father had always worked for his grandfather, old Mr. Wakely had always been nice about letting Bill come to their house and letting her go to Bill's house.

The deer came closer to the water's edge across the river. Its large ears were twitching; his big, liquid brown eyes were studying them. Bill laughed. "He wants chow," Bill explained. "I guess to him I'm a pretty good guy. But I guess if the hotel was built he'd abandon me for the tourists. I guess that's just nature."

"Bill?"

"Yes?"

"You're wrong to think as you do. I know, Bill, you were hurt back there in the store. But look at their side, Bill. Mining isn't easy. What do they do when they're unable to take the grind? You have to think of that."

"We treat our workers fine. They get benefits of all kinds. They get pensions when they retire, they get help when they're sick, they get — "

A hail interrupted, the very powerful hail of his big, angry grandfather. Mr. Wakely came striding down the slope. Under their shaggy brows his brown eyes were flashing. "Bill," he roared, "get over to Montgomery and give this note to Pierce."

He thrust an envelope into Bill's hand, and Bill, although annoyed, gave Evalin a quick smile and hurried away.

Silas P. Wakely sat down. He ran an impatient hand through his bristly beard, glared down at the roistering, frothy river. "They go too far," he said. "I'm not that old, young lady. I came to this country before they were even born, most of 'em, and no one is stealing it from me."

He was like an old bear at bay, and his rage was so intense it awed her and kept her very quiet on the bench beside him.

"Shut up!" he roared.

"Yes, sir."

"Girl," he said, and he could have been an older, more tired Bill, "I don't understand business as it's done these days. In the old days we fought fair and square, out in the open, and I've beaten men flat in my time and I've been beaten flat, too, but the fights were always fair and square. I never stole."

"Yes, sir."

"This Jackson. He's at your motel. You must've gotten a chance to know him. What's he like. Slippery, eh?"

"No, sir."

"The slippery weasel type, eh? Well, he's come to the wrong country."

The question couldn't be contained. Evalin took a deep breath, and made the plunge. "What's he done, sir?"

"That weasel's challenging my ownership of all the Blue Slide country! That pup's written me to say he'll buy half at fifty dollars an acre or take me into court to prove I'm not entitled to an inch of it."

Evalin's eyes bulged.

"But that's ridiculous!"

Silas P. Wakely shouted: "That pup is insane!"

"But why on earth would he even make such a statement? Surely he knows you can easily prove you own it all."

Silas P. Wakely frowned. "Something is fishy," he said. "I've looked into that young pup's affairs, don't think I haven't. He's a lot of things, but he isn't stupid and he isn't crazy. And don't tell me I've just contradicted myself. I know I have. It doesn't matter. So what does he think he has, eh?"

Evalin didn't know why, but she suddenly had the impression there were wheels within wheels. She stared across the river. The deer had bounded off, naturally, frightened by this big, angry, thundering old bear of a man. She wished the deer would come back. It had been beauty, a beauty she'd always found in Thorpe and which she'd always loved. Now the day wasn't beautiful and she had the uneasy notion that life in Thorpe wouldn't be peaceful for a while, and she began to wish she'd stayed up at the motel.

8

IT was Mr. Miller, the owner and publisher and one-man staff of the *Bullet* who explained the situation to Evalin in terms that made sense. He came to the motel a week or so later, ostensibly to convince Evalin that a regular weekly ad in his paper would do her more good than harm. But he didn't discuss this business very long. After he'd made his sales talk and she'd said "no," he gave a shrug of his shoulders and announced: "Well, I guess it doesn't matter. I guess that when the hotel's built I'll get all the ads I can use."

She eyed his wizened face sharply. "Do you think it will be built?"

"Yup."

"Why?"

"Because a lot of folks around here want it to be built. You know what

Wakely's fighting for, don't you?"

"What?"

"To remain the king-pin. I don't blame him, in a way. To Wakely this valley and all the surrounding mountains are his. He discovered 'em. Whatever this valley is now is because of him. I guess that maybe I'd feel the same way he does, I don't know."

The inevitable question rose in Evalin's mind. But she did the expected, first. She made old Mr. Miller a good cup of strong coffee and she cut him a thick wedge of her home-made apple pie. Because the May day was warm, she put coffee and pie on a tray and had him follow her outdoors to the porch. It wasn't quiet outdoors. A number of the guests were having a horseshoe pitching contest on the court near the creek. The clang of metal upon metal was harsh; the shouts that arose from contestants and spectators alike were disturbing. Yet it was cooler on the deep porch, and Mr. Miller smiled his pleasure, and she decided the shift of location had been a good idea. She sat down and crossed her legs and let the breezes blow on her hot, flushed face.

"Do you think," she asked at last, "that Mr. Jackson will get that Blue Slide area?"

"Could be."

"But I thought Mr. Wakely's claims to it had been upheld in court."

"What court?"

"Why, right here in the county."

"Drake says the whole thing was funny. Drake says they admitted a lot of proof that really wasn't proof. I guess Drake should know."

"But why would Mr. Jackson want to build the hotel there?"

"I guess any place will suit him, as long as it's in Thorpe. There's a smart man, Evalin. Notice how he's got Wakely on the defense already? You'd think it would be the other way around, huh?"

Down the right-hand line of cabins a door opened and Charles Jackson himself came outdoors. He wore gray flannel trousers and a white sports shirt. His glossy black hair was brushed back neatly over his well-modeled head and it came to Evalin, with a jolt, that he was quite a good-looking man, this businessman from San Antonio, Texas. As he looked toward them she waved and gestured him over. It interested her to see how eagerly he hurried over.

She got up and waved him into her chair, the skirt of her yellow cotton dress stirring in the breeze. "Want some coffee and pie, Mr. Jackson? It's your turn to be spoiled, I think."

His blue eyes twinkled. "I was wondering if my turn would come."

He turned to Mr. Miller and explained: "These folks excel at public relations. Before you can think this is merely a crass commercial enterprise, you're suddenly honored by an invitation to sit with the family in the kitchen. Or you're given a treat you don't have to pay for. It's a very interesting and very welcome and very shrewd piece of business chicanery."

Evalin chuckled and fetched more coffee and pie from the kitchen. A great cheer arose from the people down near the creek. That reminded her of something. She eyed Mr. Jackson squarely. "How come you never join in the games, Mr. Jackson? And I notice you've not once asked to borrow a horse. You're welcome to one, you know. It's included in your rent."

His black brows came together. "But that's foolish. How do you make money operating a business this way?"

"We do. Of course, our investment here was very small. Dad got the land for about ten dollars an acre. He built the cabins himself. We maintain them ourselves and — "

"Still it's legitimate business practise to charge for horses, for extras."

Evalin didn't argue it with him. She supposed that an important businessman such as Charles Jackson would laugh if she were to say the Meekers believed they were doing very well.

He scrutinized her smiling, amiable

face. He took the hint and turned his attention to the pie and coffee. For a few minutes there was reasonable quiet while both men munched and drank, and then Mr Miller wiped his lips with a paper napkin and asked bluntly:

"Anything for my paper, Mr. Jackson? I guess you know darned well I came here to question you."

Charles Jackson pursed his lips. "No, nothing that I know of, Mr. Miller. Our attitude is still the same. We think a hotel and a vacation resort would give everyone here an opportunity to make some money. We think we would make money, too. So naturally I intend to fight it out here if it takes all summer. I doubt it will, however. What do the people around here have in the way of possible employment? People who are unable to work for the mines have to take jobs in Montgomery thirty miles away over difficult and treacherous mountain roads. They know what they have now and what they have to do now. They know that until other business comes to their valley they'll have to spend their working lives outside the valley. Naturally, they resent that. And I think in the end their resentment will crystalize into solid support of me."

Mr. Miller was attentive, but not impressed. Small-town newspaperman though he was, he had a true reporter's instinct for a story. "What I meant," he said, "is what will you do about it when Mr. Wakely gets the building commission of the county to deny you a permit?"

Evalin's golden head snapped back. That device hadn't occurred to her, and as her eyes darted to Charles Jackson's face she wondered if it had occurred to him. Apparently it had not. He looked astonished, as though he couldn't quite believe such a thing were possible. But he quickly hid this astonishment behind a young, very agreeable laugh and murmured: "Oh, I don't think he can do that."

"He can, Mr. Jackson."

"How?"

"He can claim such a business would interfere with the mining and shipping operations he conducts. He can claim that unless he's given complete freedom to operate the old way he can't keep the mines going. Then the commission has to decide what's best for Thorpe. And I guess the commission would vote to support him."

"Not if it's demonstrable that my activities won't conflict with his."

"Maybe that would take a lot of doing, Mr. Jackson."

"Probably it would," Charles Jackson conceded. He was silent for several minutes and Evalin felt sorry for him because it was so apparent his position was a very weak position at best.

Abruptly, he said to Mr. Miller: "Thanks for giving me the news. I appreciate the gesture, sir."

Little, wizened Mr. Miller nodded his bald head. "I guess that's the job of a reporter, Mr. Jackson, to collect the news and to report the news. You sure you got nothing I can print?"

The tall, well-built Charles Jackson stood up, too. "I don't know. Suppose you let me telephone you this evening. This has come as a surprise to me, of course. I imagine I'll have a statement to make, but I can't guarantee that."

"Suits me, Mr. Jackson. I guess maybe I'd better tell you this. I'm on your side. I won't misrepresent facts or distort facts, because newspapers can't be run that way. But in my editorials I'll support you. And a lot of others will support you, too, and I think that maybe if Wakely tries to work against you through the building commission, you'd be smart to hire Drake as a lawyer, say, and think about getting folks to sign some sort of a petition."

"I see."

Now Mr. Miller also got to his feet. He said in his deliberate way: "I have a lot of respect for old Si Wakely. I came here just a few years after he opened up this area, and I tell you honestly this was a wilderness

125

and that Wakely deserves credit for just about all that's been accomplished here. So I've got nothing against him personally. It's just that, as I see it, his type went out of style along with a lot of things years ago. If it was a question of him being ruined by your ideas I'd back him a hundred percent, because if the pioneer can't make money it's unfair. But he's made his, and I don't think he'll be hurt except that he won't have the power he used to have. Well, power's all right so long as it doesn't keep a lot of other folks from making money and getting ahead. Since he'd prevent all that now . . . you understand, Mr. Jackson?"

He nodded shortly. "I understand. And I appreciate this, Mr. Miller."

"Good. But to keep my support, young feller, you'll have to earn it. If your plans are what you say they are, I'll do my best for you in the paper. If they're not, I'll come down on you hard."

"Fair enough, Mr. Miller."

The old man grinned crookedly at Evalin. "He sounds pretty nice, huh? Maybe we'll get something worthwhile here after all, huh?"

He gave her a little swat on the shoulder and thanked her for the pie and coffee and drove off in his old Dodge sedan. When he'd turned left through the gateposts near the creek, Evalin got the dishes and trays together and started back into the house. But Charles Jackson stopped her. He asked, almost boyishly: "Would you care to go riding with me, Miss Meeker? I'm tired of business. I'd like to get a look at some of this scenery. From the back of a horse, preferably."

She was tempted. It had been too long since she'd gone for a real ride in the mountains. But there was office work to do, and afterward she'd have to officiate as life-guard for the first swim of the season in the hot-springs pool out back. She shook her head sadly. "Sometime soon, Mr. Jackson, that would be fun. But this is my busy day, I'm afraid."

"My misfortune, of course."

She swung the door open and stepped into the house. He followed her as far as the living-room and sat down in there so gloomily she felt sorry for him. "Come on back into the kitchen, Mr. Jackson. I don't think you've sat in there before."

"Oh, I think I'd better just sit here and think. You know, Wakely has a gimmick there, an interesting gimmick."

The telephone rang in her office. Evalin excused herself and answered it, and again it was Andrew.

"I'm coming over," he snapped. "This whole thing is ridiculous."

Evalin carefully made her tones very breezy. "Oh, what a shame, Andrew. I've just agreed to go riding with Mr. Jackson. But what about some other time real soon?"

She heard the chair squeak across the hall in the living-room. But she heard nothing over the wire, for several moments, but the hum of the electric current.

"I see," Andrew presently said. "I don't suppose you'll change your mind if I ask you to?"

"I'm afraid I couldn't Andrew. But why don't you come over anyway? Dr. Zane seems a bit lonely."

"That's a dirty crack!"

"It wasn't intended to be."

"She's a fine woman, and you have no grounds for suggesting that she's the cause of our quarrel."

"I wasn't making that suggestion, Andrew."

"If I've seen her more than I should the fault is yours. You're so tied up with that motel that — "

"Let's marry, Andrew?"

"You know darned well that's impractical!"

"Why is it?"

"I've just begun, that's why. I'm not established. I may be before this fuss with Jackson is over, but until then I have to buckle down to work."

Its nakedness appalled Evalin. She gasped. And hearing her gasp, Andrew Pierce suddenly realized what he'd said. He added lamely: "When I prove that I can defend the legitimate business interests of this county, I'll have won my spurs. That's all that I meant, Evalin."

"You should be ashamed!"

"I don't know what you're talking about. Evalin, you've been very strange lately."

"Or perhaps you've been?"

"I challenge you to name one instance of that, Evalin."

She didn't bother to. Pale and trembling with fury, she hung up. She forgot about Charles Jackson out in the living-room. She hurried upstairs and sat down on her bed and glared out one of the gabled windows. So he had been Silas Wakely's man all along.

9

IT scared Andrew Pierce, but it didn't scare Silas P. Wakely. "Even the best of us blunder," the old man growled, "and it doesn't make any difference because sooner or later it would've come out anyway."

Andrew remained scared. The timing had been poor. At the proper time such a revelation would have helped him considerably. He could have posed as the champion of the untutored, the gullible. While waging the good fight for the Wakely interests, he could have seemed to be waging the good fight for the better interests of the county, and by the time Charles Jackson had been routed the name Andrew Pierce would have been synonymous with duty well done. Several years hence he'd have been a good bet for nomination to an important state job. But as it was, with

Evalin knowing the truth —

The brown eyes stabbed at his face. The bristly beard stirred, and Silas P. Wakely growled on. "How much does she know?"

"Nothing else, sir."

"How do you know she knows that?"

Andrew said candidly: "I was pretty blunt. I tried to cover up, but it was hasty and lame."

"Not that I'm angry, young fellow, but a district attorney of all people should know the importance of being very careful."

"I was angry."

"No one should ever become angry. Anger makes a man careless. When you're careless you defeat yourself."

"I realize that, sir." Andrew hesitated, wondering how best to go about the business of salvaging something from the wreckage. He added hopefully: "Of course, it's just her word against mine."

Grimly, the old man laughed.

Andrew's cheeks went hot. He got

up and walked over to the fireplace and peered down at the hearth. He heard wind in the flue and he wondered if it were still raining. He supposed it was: a thunderstorm so early in the year always left rainclouds behind it, and probably all the rivers and creeks would be running high tomorrow. He was glad that the heat wave was over; yet he wished it weren't still raining, because he wanted to make one more attempt to convince Evalin he'd not meant what she'd thought he'd meant ten days ago on the telephone. A ride to her beloved mountains, he thought, a nice picnic lunch and several kisses ought to finish the business nicely. But with the rain teeming down, and all the forests dripping . . . he sighed.

"It wouldn't work," Mr. Wakely said. "Your word against hers would leave you discredited. That girl's been raised in Thorpe. Everyone knows her. Everyone would believe her, and don't ever doubt that for a minute."

"But — "

"You're a Johnny-come-lately. And everyone remembers Drake. You'd be laughed at and you might even be impeached, and if that was started I couldn't help you a single bit."

Andrew whirled.

"Relax," snapped Silas P. Wakely. "Those are facts. I don't think you will be impeached if you use your intelligence. I'm just mentioning the possibilities."

A sudden joke made him laugh uproariously.

Andrew, puzzled, returned to the red leather armchair.

"Youngster," roared Silas P. Wakely, "you college men make me laugh. You get a certificate saying you're smart. But it's a fellow without the certificate who has to dig you out of the mess you've made for yourself. That's comical."

Andrew's lips compressed into a tight line. His brown hair wind-blown, his hazel eyes troubled and guilty, he bore little resemblance to the shrewd, poised, acute, resourceful district attorney he'd been throughout the murder trial back in March. Now he did look young, and extremely, pathetically vulnerable.

Observing this, Mr. Wakely thumped the walnut desk with his fist. "All right," he said, "I'll stop riding you. It's done. Now we'll dig you out of it. You don't love the girl, you never have, eh?"

Andrew's head came up.

"You were infatuated, sure you were. And maybe if Helen Zane hadn't come along you'd have married the girl. But you listen to an old man, young fellow. If you'd ever been in love with Evalin Meeker you'd never even have noticed Zane. When my wife was alive I never knew other women existed. So you don't love the girl and that makes it simple."

"Listen, sir — "

"Simple, because by giving Zane a heavy rush you'll be natural. You'll probably convince even me, young fellow."

The hazel eyes narrowed. "But — "

Andrew's mouth clamped shut at that point.

Silas P. Wakely nodded grimly. "Yes," he said, "you've got it. A jealous girl is apt to make all sorts of ridiculous accusations. So people have always thought, at any rate, and so people will think now."

Andrew thought it over. "I see. But suppose I love her, Mr. Wakely?"

"Then I would say, Mr. District Attorney, that the next few months will be painful to you. I don't intend to permit that business to be established in Thorpe. I would order you to follow my instructions to the letter. If you fail to do so — but there, why discuss unpleasantness? Pierce, I have great hopes for you. I think I would like to have a loyal man like you in a high office in the state government. Would you be interested, Pierce?"

With some embarrassment, Andrew

in turn asked a question. "Does a poor but ambitious man have any choice, Mr. Wakely?"

The old man grinned. "I'm glad to see," he said, "that we understand one another. Thank you for coming, Pierce. Thank you very much, very much . . . "

★ ★ ★

Mrs. Sarah Caldwell, on the other hand, didn't understand her star boarder at all. After a week of watching him go out night after night for a date with the eastern doctor, Mrs. Sarah Caldwell waylaid him. "Mr. Pierce," she smiled, "I want to have a chat with you in the living-room."

Andrew looked at the clock. It was very late. He had a crowded calendar to deal with come tomorrow, and he was tired and yearning for sleep. But he wasn't impatient with Mrs. Caldwell. She'd been nice to him from the day he'd appeared in Thorpe. She was good about looking after his clothes and seeing to it that he ate properly. Until he married, a woman such as Mrs. Caldwell had her uses, and he was intelligent enough to understand that and conceal his impatience to get to bed.

"Nice of you to wait up for me," he grinned. "But listen, it's after midnight and we should both be in bed. Won't it keep until tomorrow?"

"I don't think you're being wise, Mr. Pierce. I know that Dr. Zane is very sweet and attractive and charming, but she is on vacation, you see, and when she leaves Thorpe you and Evalin Meeker will still be here."

Andrew went into the small living-room. Grimacing, he took one of the overstuffed chairs. "Well, say it all," he told her. "I always listen to you, don't I?"

Flattered, Sarah Caldwell sat down. "As I see it, Mr. Pierce, things are stirring in Thorpe. I got something in the mail just this morning, for instance.

There's a committee being formed to push this hotel idea that Mr. Jackson has in mind. I'm wanted to serve on that committee."

"Don't join it," he said quickly. "Strictly between us, Mrs. Caldwell, Jackson and his crowd are dishonest. I can't say more at this time, but just you remember that."

"He is? That nice young man? Why, I can hardly believe that! You must be wrong. He has such a sweet, friendly face."

"All confidence men do," Andrew said sadly. "That's why they're able to operate. You wouldn't believe anything a man said if that man had a sinister face and shifty eyes, would you?"

Mrs. Caldwell was indignant. "I always say that a person who can't meet your eyes is a person you can't trust. I wasn't born yesterday, Mr. Pierce."

Andrew laughed agreeably. He stood up, handsome in his stocky way in a tweed suit and a dull maroon knit necktie. "Well, that's my point, Mrs. Caldwell. That's why the successful confidence men are men who are as sweet to look at as Mr. Charles Jackson — to use your adjective."

"Why, bless my soul, I never thought of that."

Thinking he'd nicely distracted her, Andrew gave her shoulder a playful swat and headed for the door.

Her voice stopped him cold.

"Anyway," Mrs. Caldwell said, "I don't understand you, Mr. Pierce. You run around with that doctor, and while you're doing that Evalin is running around with Mr. Jackson."

Andrew turned softly, his mind milling. "Oh?"

"And I'm worried," said the forthright Mrs. Caldwell. "You've had a quarrel, I know that. And I'm worried lest this quarrel interfere with this love that was surely made in heaven."

"But — "

"He's so handsome and quick and merry and friendly, Mr. Pierce. Why, if

140

you hadn't told me he was a thief — "

"I didn't say that!"

Mrs. Caldwell gasped. "Why, that reminds me! Mrs. Laursen told me just this afternoon she was going to sign that petition the committee's getting out. I'd better tell her he's a thief."

Perspiring, Andrew got between her and the telephone. "Will you listen?" he demanded. "I can't prove that right now. I just gave you a friendly warning, Mrs. Caldwell."

"You can't prove it?" Her little black eyes grew perplexed. "But if you can't prove it why do you call him a thief?"

Wearily, Andrew said he was sorry he'd used the term. He retracted it. He told her that if he couldn't give a deeply treasured friend a friendly warning without being misquoted all over town, then he was sorry he'd ever started it.

This, at last, did distract Mrs. Caldwell. "I understand," she said. "He is a thief but he isn't a thief, so there."

Routed, Andrew went to bed. But now he couldn't sleep. He thought of Evalin riding through the mountains with Charles Jackson and he thought of how much fun she could be on such occasions and he began to wonder about himself and Dr. Zane. Was she serious, or was she just flirting?

★ ★ ★

The following evening he was handsomer and livelier than Dr. Helen Zane had ever seen him. He slammed his car door shut with a flourish and came whistling up the little path of her cabin down by the creek. "Lovely," he pronounced her, "simply lovely."

His lips stormed hers.

Dr. Helen Zane suddenly went warm and breathless.

He was grinning proudly when he released her. "Didn't think I had the nerve, did you?" he teased. "Well, where do we go tonight?"

Dr. Zane recovered her poise.

Attractive in a light gray flannel suit, she opened her handbag and took out her mirror and surveyed her lips. She gave a mock frown.

"That was mean," she told him. "I spent half an hour getting my lipstick just so."

His hazel eyes went serious. "Does it really matter?"

She flushed.

"We could eat at that steakhouse in Mongomery," he said, bridging the awkward silence. He jingled the change in his pocket. "First of the month means pay day, and I'm feeling rich. You can eat the biggest steak you want."

But a hail came from Mr. Linden several cabins up the line. He was, it developed, having trouble with his necktie. His pop eyes smoldering, he marched over to Helen Zane. "I don't know why I agreed to go," he said. "It's all foolishness. Anyhow, it shouldn't be a dress-up occasion."

"We promised Evalin, didn't we? I

should think you'd be glad to do her a favor."

"I don't need to be told my duty as a friend."

Very skillfully, Helen Zane knotted the tie and slid the knot up between the points of his white shirt-collar. "There," she smiled. "And if it weren't for Andrew here I'd be proud to be escorted by you."

"At least," he bragged tartly, "you'd be with a man of principle."

Mr. Linden marched back to his cabin, small and stooped, scrawny and partially bald, but an impressive dapper figure of a wizened oldster for all that.

Helen Zane laughed softly, a pleasant contralto laugh that seemed to suit the pleasant June evening. "The little old rip," she said fondly. "The Meekers have fine guests, Andrew, did you know that?"

His conscience pricked, made his voice edgy. "Am I supposed to enjoy being told I lack principle?"

The gray eyes in the lovely face

sobered. "I know," she said, "I know. I feel like two cents, too. I almost checked out this morning. I mean this, Andrew. I love her parents very much — they're so genuine. And I like her, too, silly, mixed-up kid that she is. But — "

"Where did he think you were going, Helen?"

Little furrows marred the creamy tan symmetry of her forehead. "Oh, didn't you hear? Some people have decided they'll support Charles Jackson in this fuss that's going on. So they're holding a meeting, and Evalin's invited us to attend, and we all agreed to, naturally."

"Naturally?"

"Andrew, she does all sorts of things for us. Why shouldn't we do her a favor?"

He sat down, all the liveliness going out of him. He asked bluntly: "Does she believe Jackson stands a chance?"

"Yes."

"Why?"

But this didn't interest the lovely doctor from New Jersey. "Oh, who knows?" she laughed. "Personally, I don't really care. If we leave in a hurry we'll get back to Thorpe in time for the meeting."

He got up and led her up the path to his car. He swung it around the loop and nosed it out between the gateposts. He was silent for several minutes, guiding the car through the little flurry of traffic in the heart of the village, easing it over the bumps of the dirt road that offered a short cut to the state highway. He sighed and settled back on the seat as the car purred over the smooth, wide road. "Nice evening," he said presently. "Don't you love the mountains, Helen?"

"They're very beautiful, of course. See how they roll mile after mile like the waves of a cherry red sea!"

Some of the peaks did seem to be swimming in the sunset's glow, he noticed, and down in the gorges violet evening shadows had gathered, and soon they'd come rising darkly to blot everything but the stars from sight.

"But I couldn't live in this country," Dr. Helen Zane said. "I have a vest-pocket estate I love, Andrew. The reason I came out here was that I'd been disappointed in what I thought was love. I never expected to remain out here, and of course I won't."

"I see. It didn't occur to me that you were rich."

"Andrew?"

"Yes?"

"I'm not rich enough to buy you, Andrew. I think that you should know that."

He looked at her angrily. "Do you think I can be bought?"

"In your present frame of mind, Andrew, yes."

He looked back at the road just in time to avoid a crash with a truck that had come rumbling around a curve.

"But that attitude will pass," Dr. Helen Zane said. "If I weren't sure of that, Andrew, I'd not be with you now."

"Listen — "

"No, Andrew. Talking doesn't help. Time will take care of it, I think. Now, then, shall we be man and woman sallying off to an exciting date?"

"Actually," he said, "I'm right about Jackson. And if Evalin's trying a game, she will be sorry."

"I doubt it," Helen announced. "I really doubt that very, very much."

Andrew shook his head. He wished that some time during the past few weeks he'd been able to take Evalin for a picnic in one of her beloved forests. What they needed to do, he continued to think, was to have a talk . . .

10

AT the fateful meeting that night in quaint Community Hall, the interested public was treated to a rousing speech by no less a personage than the President of the Jackson International Business Development Corporation. He made a fine appearance on the little stage with the spotlight full on his face. He wasn't at all nervous, smiling and talking as though it were perfectly natural for him to be up there talking to a roomful of strangers. Evalin, listening and watching, began to think there was much, much more to Charles Jackson than met the eye at the motel. At the motel he was just another pleasant young fellow who could sit talking or playing silly card games as though he had nothing more important on his mind than killing time. But there on the stage, a handsome man in his gray slacks and tweed sport jacket, he was all business and fighting heart. He established that the moment he'd told the preliminary jokes all public speakers, for some reason or another, seemed to think were vitally necessary. As the last gale of laughter died down he stated bluntly: "I am not here to beg, ladies and gentlemen. The corporation I represent has holdings all over the world — profitable, I might add, and so there's no reason for me to beg. I think I can make money here. I think you can make money when I establish the hotel and vacation resort, and so this is a business proposition for you as well as for me, and if you go along with me that's fine and if you don't I'll build the hotel and resort somewhere else. Is that understood? I will locate here only if the majority wants me to locate here and if money is put up to demonstrate the support is genuine and permanent."

He paused as if to observe the effect.

Noticing the intense silence, he smiled grimly. "Yes," he resumed. "It will cost you money. It will cost you so much a share, or it will cost you so much in terms of credit extended to us. There's no reason why it shouldn't cost you money. You all know what would happen if a hundred or so tourists spent ten months out of the year here. Your businesses would boom, you would have security and you would have jobs to offer the people who now have to go to Montgomery to get them. You see? I'm not asking you for money, just as I'm not asking for your support. If you want me, fine; those are my terms. If you don't I'll accept an offer I have elsewhere in this corner of Colorado."

It came from a fellow at the rear of the hall. "How much money would you nccd bcforc you'd believe we mean business?"

"Ten thousand," Charles Jackson snapped. "If the hotel is built you're in for a share of the profits. If it isn't built the money will be refunded."

There were buzzing sounds, the sounds of people whispering and mumbling with excitement. Evalin was interested to notice that no one seemed surprised by the demand for cash support. Equally surprising was the fact that no one got up to attack that demand.

Charles Jackson laughed boyishly. "Fine," he said. "Now that we understand one another, I'll tell you what I have in mind for Thorpe. I have in mind a vacation resort that will be publicized nationally and internationally just as Aspen is, just as Sun Valley is, just as Palm Springs is. I won't build in the expectation of making a fortune overnight. But I will build in the expectation of making a fortune over a period of years, and I think that the sooner we get the building done the sooner we'll all have extra incomes to spend as we wish. That being so, I've worked out a program and a schedule. I want a permit to build, and a license to operate in this area. Then I want land, about twenty acres of land in a scenic setting. I'll pay five hundred an acre for it, no more. With, be it understood, the ten thousand I will insist upon having before I spend so much as a penny of the corporation's money. Ten — "

He never got farther. For that was when Bill Wakely stood up at last and bawled the argument Evalin had been expecting him to bawl.

"Afraid to risk your own money, Jackson? What sort of business proposition is this? What you're asking is for land and ten thousand, I've got that straight. But what are you putting up?"

"A hotel, a vacation resort, Mr. Wakely. And, I might add, despite the opposition of your grandfather and you."

Bill laughed loudly. He strode up the center aisle toward the stage, a big, brawny man still in work clothes and with his Stetson shoved back on his head. He hopped nimbly up to the stage and his brown eyes swept the audience. "Before you support a guy with an offer like that," he said, "listen to this: so far all he's doing is promising. But every one of you here would be risking his money and the nice way of life we have here. For what? Maybe a fortune. But maybe not a fortune, either."

"That's for them to decide," Charles Jackson pointed out.

"I'm just mentioning the risk you didn't mention," Bill said. "I've got that right, since most of the folks here either work for us or get their livings because of us."

"Is that a threat, Mr. Wakely?"

Bill laughed. "Nope, Mr. Jackson. Just a warning to you, that's all, that the Wakelys look after the interests of their friends and employees. Go ahead and make the rest of your speech."

"Shall I tell them your grandfather offered me five thousand to clear out?"

Bill gaped.

The audience gasped.

And that was the moment the good-looking Texan struck.

"There it is," he said briskly. "I won't say another word because I'm not here to beg. It's up to you to figure out what you want to do. I'll stay around here until the end of June. If you want the hotel I'll know by then. If you don't I'll take the five thousand and breeze on."

"That's a lie!" shouted Bill Wakely. "That's a dirty lie!"

Charles Jackson just shrugged and came down from the stage. He came over to Evalin and smiled faintly. "Ready to go back home, Miss Meeker? I did promise your folks not to keep you out late."

Evalin hurried outdoors with him. "Was that the truth? About the offer, I mean?"

Charles Jackson waved her into his car. "It was the truth. I'm surprised he was so generous. He has me blocked, unless I can convince you or someone else that selling me twenty acres will be a big help to this community."

"Then you weren't just joking that night you offered me double whatever Mr. Wakely had offered me?"

"No."

"But you never followed that offer up."

"It would've been poor strategy." He gazed up at the starry sky. The Milky Way was very clear and several planets appeared to be so close their flame would come smashing down on a mountain peak. "Bill Wakely's strategy just now was poor," he said. "See what happens if your strategy is poor?"

He started the car and backed it out of the parking lot into the street. He swung left and headed back toward the motel on the western outskirts of the village. "By the way," he said, "I don't think he knew of the offer. To be fair and honest, I think he was as surprised as everyone else."

Evalin had a memory, suddenly, of an enraged old man shouting that he'd draw blood before he was dragged down. It made her shiver. Such a man, she thought, wouldn't hesitate to use his money if he could.

"It's interesting," Charles Jackson said. "Inevitably, I wonder what Mr. Wakely is afraid of. I won't damage him. To say that I will just doesn't make sense. How can I? In what way would a tourist trade hurt him? Do you hurt him?"

"He wants the control, I think. To him, really, all this valley is his. None of us is rich enough to challenge his control. You might be, I don't know."

The car labored up the grade. Charles Jackson shifted down a gear, and when they reached an observation turnoff he swung from the road and braked the car. He looked not at Evalin but down at the valley below. Within its bowl of mountains and with lights shining on every street corner and in most of the houses, it made a lovely sight, and he noticed that, and he laughed.

"That's why you stay here, Miss Meeker, isn't it?"

"Haven't I told you to call me Evalin? We don't stand on ceremony here, Mr. Jackson."

"I'm Chuck. Lots of Charleses are called Chuck, but I got the nickname because that's what I did in college. Texas football, Evalin, is a wide-open game of forward passes. I was pretty good at throwing them, so they began to call me Chuck."

"You've had quite a life, Chuck, haven't you?"

"Quite a life. From a place very much like this, one night, I watched a girl kiss a fellow on the Meping River in Siam. There's a lot in that, Evalin. Wherever you go people are the same and the world's the same, so you have quite a life, really, just about anywhere."

She agreed. She, too, she recalled, had had 'quite a life' even if she'd never left the mountains long enough to feel lonesome for them. Once, high up in the mountains, she'd seen a wild brown bear with her cubs. Another time, high up in the mountains, she'd been all alone with drifting plump flakes of snow and she'd watched that snow transform the mountain-world into a glistening fairy-land of white. And another time . . .

"Evalin?"

"Yes?"

"Will you sell me that land?"

"No."

"Why not?"

"I expect to build a home there. I expect to raise my children there."

"I see. Andrew Pierce's children? Or Bill Wakely's?"

"I answered your question, Chuck."

"The reason I asked about the land is this: I can give old Mr. Wakely a scare, but I can't get the Blue Slide. Even if I could get the Blue Slide I wouldn't take it as a gift, please understand, but — "

"Then why fight for it?"

"I'm not."

"But according to him — "

"I'm just feinting, of course. The

159

idea was to make him forget about your twenty acres. Clever?"

She supposed it was.

"But of course," he said, "if you won't sell I'll have to work some other trick. I hoped you would sell."

She understood, and she thought that if she did sell it would probably be to a person like him rather than to Silas Wakely. Sold to Silas Wakely, it would be a tract of land without meaning, simply another patch of earth he'd add to many patches of earth and allow to remain idle and useless for as long as he lived. But sold to Charles Jackson, it would be land that would give pleasure to many and it would indirectly enrich the village, too.

He reached out, gave her arm a quick squeeze. "It's all right, Evalin. This will astonish you, but I can understand reserving a piece of land for your personal use some day. I have such a holding. It's in Texas, Evalin, and that's the sweetest land I know. It's range. For as far as the eye can see in any direction it's range — not most of it mine, of course, but I can see and enjoy all of it from mine and it means much to me. On that land and under that sky and with that view, I always feel happier than I do anywhere else and — well, no more pitch for your land. I take you seriously, and I hope you take me seriously, when I say I wish you much happiness on your special corner of earth."

He fell silent, leaving her with a quivery sensation and goose-pimples on her arms. She gave him a sidelong glance and saw in the moonlight and starlight that his face, cleanly modeled and amiable and handsome, was tender with understanding and emotion.

"Thanks," she said. "That was very nice, Chuck."

"Well, shall we get to the motel?"

"You understand, don't you, that I want you to build that hotel and resort? It has nothing to do with wanting to get back at Andrew Pierce, either."

He laughed softly. "Now there's a

strange romance. I mind my business, generally, but what ever made you think you were in love with a fellow like him?"

"I am in love with him."

"Bunk. Just plain bunk. Listen to me, Miss Evalin Meeker. I see a great deal, I hear a great deal. I don't miss the sugary way you talk to Zane, and I don't miss the sugary way Zane talks to you. Very civilized, eh? A recognition of civilized women that each has the right to the love she wants if she can win it fairly and squarely, eh?"

Evalin was stung. It was one thing to discuss land and her feeling about land with him. It was another thing for him to have the audacity to discuss Andrew with her.

"Would you prefer," she asked acidly, "to see us clobbering one another with clubs?"

"It would be more natural."

"Apparently we're more civilized in Colorado than you are in Texas!"

"And," he said, as though she'd not

spoken, "it would be more convincing, too."

"Am I supposed to be convincing *you*, Mr. Jackson?"

"That part of me that forms a segment of the world in which you live, yes. Shall I tell you another reason you don't convince me or any more experienced person?"

"I want to go home!"

"Certainly. One thing about Texans, though, they have more courage than you. They can take the truth."

"What is the truth?"

"You were shocked by a disclosure Andrew Pierce made to you. Since then you've seen a lot of Bill Wakely and quite a bit of me. Why were you so shocked?"

"He should be ashamed. He's doing Mr. Wakely's bidding and — "

She caught herself, scowled. She lost her temper.

"That was very clever of you, wasn't it?"

"No. I had that information long

before you did, Evalin. In fact, I have a letter from Andrew Pierce dated away back in February. In response to an inquiry I sent him he gave himself away. But what I meant was this: if you're in love with a person you may be disturbed by something he does, but you're never so shocked you discard him just like that. You would discard a person you didn't love, but not a person you did love, and shall I tell you why?"

"Why?"

"Because ladies aren't that way, Evalin, and you're a lady. If a lady loves she sticks to the fellow she loves until the bitter end. You're not sticking. You're a lady. So obviously it wasn't love and it isn't love and there you are."

She was too dumbfounded to speak. In the silence he chuckled, but not with triumph, and started the car. He swung it around on the observation turn-off and shifted into second as they went on up the grade toward the motel. He drove very carefully and slowly, and she noticed that and snapped irritably: "We won't fall over the side, Mr. Jackson."

"Are we back to formality?"

"We most certainly are."

"And won't go riding any more, I imagine?"

"You don't get the land. You don't have to play up to me for it."

"Do you think I would?"

She began to say yes, but something deep within her prevented her. She knew, even though she was angry, that that would be going too far. So she contented herself with a little snort and looked off to her right across the gorge at another hill looming purple and beautiful in the night.

He stopped the car again, on another turn-off. He reached out with strong hands and suddenly drew her close. She never had the chance to stop him. His lips drove down, caught hers by surprise and held the kiss for a good ten or fifteen seconds. She went cold, then warm, then furious.

"You leave my motel!" she snapped. "You leave the instant we get there."

"Certainly. But that wasn't the kiss, Evalin, of a girl in love with Andrew Pierce. How interesting."

11

AS written up in Mr. Miller's newspaper the story of the meeting made exciting reading. Evalin discovered that Chuck and she had left the meeting much too early. The meeting had closed on a note of fireworks, as it were. Apparently stung by the revelation, Bill Wakely had stood thundering on the stage a good ten minutes. He'd denounced the supporters of "so-called progress." In effect he'd called them ingrates. In scathing terms he'd called them blind, greedy fools who would destroy the good things they had in the stupid hope of waxing fat and rich on tourists' gold. He'd pointed out that Thorpe already had a hotel and several boarding houses and even a very beautiful and efficiently operated motel. And there, he'd shouted, was the proof that the hope of waxing fat and rich on tourists' gold was stupid. "Do you see?" he'd thundered. "Do you see the Meekers riding in a fancy Cadillac? Do you see Hennessy paying off the mortgage on his hotel? Do you see Mrs. Caldwell and Mrs. Ryberly and all the other ladies who operate boarding-houses running around town all dressed up in mink? You bet you don't. And the reason is this. The tourist business isn't the big time business Jackson would have you believe. As a matter of fact — "

But there he'd been interrupted.

Someone had jumped up to shout: "Why did your Gramps try to pay him to leave town?"

Bill had lost his temper. "Anyone who says Gramps did such a thing is a liar."

Someone else had jumped up to demand: "If Jackson's so sure to lose his shirt, why's your grandfather all het up?"

"Don't you think he worries about

you people? Do you think he wants to see you lose your shirts, too?"

"If the hotel ain't built we get our money back."

"And if your Gramps worries about us so much why don't he pay decent wages?"

"You get more than you're worth, if you want to know!"

That had done it. Bill had been shouted and hooted from the platform and a president of the committee had been elected, and it had been proposed and passed that the sum demanded by Charles Jackson be collected if possible and placed into escrow as evidence of public support of the project and a vote of confidence in the young fellow who'd come to town with a business dream that could transform it.

The whole thing left Evalin somewhat breathless. She had once said to Dr. Zane that people with children and homes wanted and needed security, and that if they believed for an instant the hotel and vacation resort would bring fresh money in, create more jobs, they'd do a great deal of thinking before they supported Silas Wakely. Now the very thing she'd prophesied had come to pass, but much more quickly than she'd have believed possible and despite the very open and angry opposition of Bill as well as his grandfather! Chuck might still be frozen out. If he couldn't buy the land he needed, that would settle the matter in a hurry. But the fact remained that the dominance of the Wakelys had been challenged by the people themselves and that from now on, for better or for worse, things would be different in Thorpe.

Curious about it all, she invented an excuse for driving down into town. She parked her car under the pine before Lenore Dalton's ramshackle home and restaurant and swung the gate open and strode briskly across the yard. She made an engaging sight in her white Bermuda shorts and yellow blouse, and Andrew, coming out the door, looked at her with more interest than he'd displayed in months. Looking warm and uncomfortable himself in a brown suit, he quickly smiled and offered his hand. "Nice to see you," he said cordially. "It's been too long, Evalin, much too long."

She noticed that there were puffy half-circles under his eyes. She noticed something else about him that she'd never noticed before, that his smile was too quick, too suave and that it didn't quite reach his hazel eyes, which were somewhat calculating. But she answered the smile with a smile and dropped onto one of the porch chairs. "We're getting our share of warm weather, Andrew, aren't we? That heat wave back in May, and here's another one building up."

"The sheepherders like it. There'll be about ten thousand sheep moving through this street in a little while. I always like to see them. One cycle is ended, another cycle begins. For instance, last year at this time I was merely a struggling lawyer with a hole-in-the-wall office in Montgomery. Now I'm the district attorney. I wonder what next year will bring."

"No doubt an important job in the state government. If you defeat Chuck, of course."

"Chuck?" His brownish eyebrows formed question marks.

"Chuck. He's called Chuck because at college he excelled at throwing forward passes. Will you think it catty if I add that these passes were thrown out in the open?"

His jaw hardened. But he didn't lose his temper. "I think," he said quietly, "that you've forgotten something important."

"Such as?"

"That I was elected to protect and defend the interests of the public. The Wakelys are a part of the public, and it could be said that if I were helping merely the Wakelys I would be doing the job I'm paid to do. But I'm doing more than helping the Wakelys. I'm also helping every person in this village who is under the spell cast by this — well, I won't say confidence-man. In time you'll understand that, Evalin."

"I doubt it."

"Anyway, it doesn't matter, Evalin. If I had to do it I'd publicize some interesting things about Charles Jackson. But I won't have to do it. The Blue Slide will remain the property of Wakely. Except for your twenty acres there's no desirable site left in Thorpe. So I fancy that Jackson will be moving on and that this fuss will end in several more weeks."

"What are the interesting things about him, Andrew?"

He shook his head. He got up and started toward the porch steps. But he halted there and turned to face her and he said acidly: "Was it such a strain upon your undying love that you were unable to give me one small shred of faith, Evalin?"

"Shall I ask Lenore inside if believing in you would be justified?"

He went rigid. Hostility leaped into his eyes, and for a very brief instant there it all was to see and to understand, the truth he'd hidden perhaps even from himself. The queer thing to Evalin was that the truth didn't hurt a bit. In a sense it came as a relief to her, and before he could rage she got up and shook her lovely golden head.

"Sorry," she said crisply. "That was unfair. We were never engaged, were we? I should have realized that wasn't an oversight. You're too deliberate in everything you do to overlook anything so important."

He turned on his heel and went down the porch steps. She watched sadly as he got into his car and drove off; then she went into the house and made herself comfortable in a chair in the small, clean dining-room. Lenore, coming in, gave an exclamation of happy surprise. "Now here," she said, "is what I happen to call hitting the old jackpot. Hi, Evalin."

"Hi, Lenore."

"If you want some coffee wait a few minutes, honey. That stuff I served the D. A. was rank poison."

"No coffee. Just some buttermilk."

"See the D. A. just now?"

"Uh-huh."

Lenore disappeared into her kitchen. She returned with a glass of buttermilk and a plate of doughnuts and sat down at the table with Evalin. Her green, amiable eyes were twinkling. "I guess he rubbed you the wrong way too, huh?"

"Not really. How's business?"

"Swell. Say, if that hotel and vacation resort brings me the kind of business in the future it's already brought, I'll end up in a real house and the kid won't have to spend most of his time with his grannyfolks over in Montgomery."

"How nice."

"Since that Jackson guy eats breakfast an' lunch here, you'd be surprised how many folks keep coming in."

"Yes, a lot of people are supporting him, aren't they?"

The bright red head went up and down vigorously. But the freckled face was sad. "But a fat lot of good," said Lenore Dalton, "their support will be. Andrew was telling me they've got Mr. Jackson over a barrel. The other day it was decided Mr. Wakely has every right to Blue Slide, and there went Mr. Jackson's big chance down the drain."

Remembering what Chuck had told her, Evalin smiled. "Oh, don't be so sure, Lenore."

"And it's a dirty shame," Lenore said hotly. "Because what happens when Mr. Jackson leaves? You think the Wakelys are going to forget the names of the folks who wanted Mr. Jackson to win? I'll tell you something that'll floor you. Bill Wakely fired four fellows yesterday. They were the fellows who asked all those questions at the meeting last week."

Evalin gaped.

Lenore laughed tautly. "A real funny thing, isn't it? Every day in front of all the mines and in front of their headquarters, too, the Wakelys see to it that Old Glory goes up to the top of the flagpole. But do they believe in what that flag stands for? You hear a lot about opportunity in this country and the rights of everybody to get ahead if they can. But what do the Wakelys do? They work a fast deal like this and they do a dirty thing like that. Why, you can't even think your own thoughts in this town any more!"

Evalin stared down at the doughnuts, too dumb-founded and disturbed to speak. She picked up a doughnut and bit into it and mechanically chewed and swallowed.

"Well," said Lenore, "I guess that's why the D. A. was pleased. I guess old Wakely showed Mr. Jackson, with the D. A.'s help, and now I guess everything will be Wakely's way and Andrew's way and it all makes me sick, that's what it does."

A peculiar sound came in through the opened window. It was a high, thin, quavering murmuring that somehow sounded spooky, unreal. Then a dog barked, and suddenly dozens of dogs were barking, and the sound became recognizable to Evalin as the sound of thousands of sheep baa-ing off in the distance. She jumped to her feet, her eyes dancing. "It's summer, Lenore! Hear summer coming to our town?"

The amply curved redhead hurried out to the porch with her. Lenore called her dog and chained her dog out back, and it was a good thing that she had, for several minutes later a half-dozen goats came mincing around the corner and swung into the street, their bells tingling but their bearded faces solemn with their heavy responsibility. About fifty feet behind them came the first of the baa-ing sheep, their tiny feet kicking up dust that went swirling in all directions on the breeze. The dust thickened, and now to the sounds of the bleating were added the sounds of thousands of feet striking on asphalt and dirt and the barkings of sheep-dogs and the rattles of pebbles in the rattle-cans the sheepherders used to transmit their orders to the lead goats. For a half-hour all was noise and confusion as the sheep marched through in their seasonal trek toward the mountains and the high summer ranges. Kids shrieked, kids ran, and sheep took fright and lambs took fright and these ran, too, posing problems for the sheep-dogs and the sheepherders as well. Only the goats seemed immune to this excitement. With aloof majesty they did their job of leading the sheep on and on along the back street, and perhaps because of their calm a reasonable good order was restored and the sea of dirty-white wool undulated on, flowing around a corner at last and taking the dust and the smells and the noise with it.

Evalin met Lenore's flashing green eyes. "What excuse did Bill give for firing those men?"

"Just that the mine didn't need them any more."

"Are they laying off men?"

"Just those four, and his statement didn't make him popular, Honey, I'll tell you that. Two of those fellows had real seniority. If it was a legit layoff, others would have been fired, not them."

And that, she thought, was what Bill had meant when he'd said that whatever his grandfather wanted done would be done by him, and not reluctantly, either. It was perfectly natural, if unfair and it would be perfectly natural if in the future Bill did even worse. He had the Wakely pride and he had the Wakely determination to keep the control which he deemed to be the Wakely right. He'd never opposed his grandfather even when his personal ambitions and dreams had been involved.

"Poor Bill," she said quietly. "He's strange, Lenore, isn't he? He's big and rough and tough. He could take care of himself just about anywhere and under any conditions. But he won't ever try the one thing he wants to try, and so there he is making an idiot of himself."

"Well, maybe not. He gets it all some day and maybe it's what he wants."

"Even if they won they'd lose, Lenore."

"Huh?"

Evalin stood up and shrugged. "They'll never have the respect they used to have if they shut Chuck out of town. And people will nurse their resentment, and no matter what happens it won't be forgotten."

"Maybe they don't care."

"Bill will care. Not Mr. Wakely, perhaps, but Bill will. As long as the mines operate he'll have to live here, you see."

Full of that thought, Evalin went back to her Morris Minor sedan. Having learned what she'd wanted to learn, she drove across town to the Wakely headquarters building near Thorpe River. She stepped into the old, musty wooden building and smiled at Sarah on duty at the small reception desk. Sarah nodded, and Evalin went down the narrow hall, knocked on Bill's door and quickly stepped into his cubbyhole office.

It was a Bill she didn't know, his face fighting mad, his brown eyes blazing. It wasn't the Bill who'd once carried her books and who'd often talked of marriage. Instead, it was a Bill who glared at her as if upon an enemy, and who then promptly bulled into an attack.

"If you sell to Jackson," he snapped, "I'll break that ore-hauling contract we have with your father."

"Shush."

"Don't you shush me. You were at that meeting. You were one of the ringleaders, in fact."

"I wasn't. I was invited to attend and I did, period."

"What's happened to people around here? You'd think that all these years we've been treating them like dirt."

"They want more than they have, Bill. Isn't that quite natural? Why do you keep on working? Because you want more than you already have."

He took off on a tangent, as he generally did when he argued with her. "You bet Gramps offered him five thousand. Gramps thought it was the cheapest way to save this town for the people who've lived in it all their lives."

"Then he wasn't a liar, Bill?"

"That guy — "

"You just romped all over him without bothering to get the facts?"

He ground his teeth. Evalin, shocked, sat down and glanced about the eight-by-ten office with its old desk and wooden furniture and big filing cabinet at the back.

"Oh, fine," she taunted. "There's a real fair man."

"Listen to me, Ev."

"Nope. You'll distort everything if you can. The knight in shining armor can't be wrong. Nor can his august father, the emperor himself."

He discovered something that made

him uneasy. He discovered that Evalin, usually sweet and amiable and quiet, was hopping and noisily mad.

"Well," she said, "you should be ashamed along with your father and Andrew. You're a bunch of greedy mavericks trying to hog the range, and heaven help anyone who wants just a taste of grass. You've corrupted Andrew, you've tried to freeze Chuck Jackson out of town, you've fired men who disagreed with you, and now you're threatening my family."

"There's only one way to fight — all out or nothing."

"With lies, with threats, with starvation? You make me sick."

"This is a darned good village. We'll keep it that way."

"No you won't. Not if I have to *give* Chuck the land."

"Don't you see what will happen? The first thing you know we won't be able to get workers. Then the tourists will complain about the noise the trucks make going through town.

Then — you come back here!"

Evalin didn't.

Quivering with indignation and fury, she hurried back to her car.

If they wanted war, she thought, they could darned well have it! Imagine firing people and threatening people just because the people refused to jump through their hoops!

12

TOM MEEKER kicked it around in his mind for about a week. He then went to Dr. Helen Zane, of all people, for a piece of impartial advice. And equally surprising was the fact that the Helen Zane, who sat down in the kitchen with them that warm late June night, wasn't a woman counseling peace. "I'd sell," she said bluntly. "I know that will create problems for you all, but you have no choice. You amputate a leg in order to save a life; and you assert your independence in order to live your own lives. It really comes down to that."

Evalin nodded. Those were her sentiments, even if she'd not been able to express them as pithily.

Tom Meeker looked at his wife. Emma Meeker, in turn, looked at Evalin. Her lively blue eyes twinkled.

"No more Andrew?" she asked.

"Mom, this isn't the time for nonsense."

"To me it always was nonsense."

"Please, Mom."

"None of this matters," Emma Meeker said firmly. "All that matters is that you've come to your emotional senses. Or haven't you?"

Dr. Zane tactfully rose and left.

Evalin glared.

Mrs. Emma Meeker just smiled on, not a whit disturbed by the glare. "When did you learn the truth about Andrew?" she asked.

"Perhaps I haven't learned whatever you're talking about."

"You wouldn't be coming out openly for Mr. Jackson, dear, if you were still intent upon marrying Andrew. This means a great deal to him, I suspect. It may put him on the road to the governor's mansion."

Evalin didn't care. As she saw it, the important thing was for them all to demonstrate they couldn't be cowed into submission. That was all that mattered to her right now. If the Wakelys won now, Thorpe would be a horrible place. The Wakelys mightn't want to take advantage of their positions, but inevitably they would, because people were that way. Now that war had been declared, it was either win or be destroyed.

She turned to her father. "Well, Dad?"

"It's pretty serious," Tom Meeker said. "I clear about seven hundred a month on that contract."

"I know."

"I've been with them for years, too. And they weren't bad years. Look at our motel. Look at you — never once in your life did you go hungry."

"And I won't ever, and you won't, either."

He exhaled gustily. It was very warm in the kitchen even with all the windows opened to the breeze. The trees stood tall and inviting in the back yard, and beyond them the mountains looked cool and inviting, too, their peaks beautifully limned against the sky by the gold of the declining sun.

"We could talk to old man Wakely, couldn't we?"

Evalin laughed. "We could. If you want to waste your time, let's pop into the car and get over there."

"And why does it have to be your land?"

"Because it's best for the purpose. And Chuck can get it. He can't get anything else."

"Just the same — "

"Tom, dear?"

He swung his gaze to his wife. And Emma Meeker was still smiling, but now her face was the face of a fighter.

"Tom," she said, "why keep her on tenterhooks? You know very well you'll take an active part in this battle."

"I do?"

"Because three of those men who were fired for speaking their minds are friends of yours. You know them well enough to know they were good workers always and that they didn't deserve the treatment they received."

He growled with righteous wrath. "I got two of them jobs. And I told old Wakely to his face he isn't the man that he used to be."

Evalin had never felt prouder of him."

She asked, her eyes shining: "What did he say, Dad?"

"He said if I cross him up I'll discover he's as tough as he ever was."

"Dad!"

"So that," he concluded, "was when I told him you'd be selling that land to Jackson."

Evalin's mouth fell agape.

So did that of her mother.

Tom Meeker chuckled. "Only reason I didn't tell you sooner," he said, "was that it happened just this afternoon, an' from the minute I got home I had to listen to women chattering like our magpies do."

A hundred and twelve pounds of laughing, excited Evalin Meeker went banging into his arms. "You old fire-eater!" she chortled. "Ma, Dad wants a bottle of cold beer!"

"His waistline!"

"The more of Dad the better, Mom. Isn't Dad just beautiful?"

Tom Meeker smoothed his raggle-taggle hair proudly. Happily, Evalin got him a bottle of cold beer.

★ ★ ★

The deed in her handbag, she drove once again into town and had a chat with Mr. Callaway in the Thorpe Land and Savings Bank. She had him draw up a bill of sale that would protect her interests if the hotel weren't built, and when he'd attended to that she had him draw a hundred dollars from her savings account. He was opposed to the whole thing, and he said so. His eyes solemn behind his eyeglasses, he produced a record of all their accounts and he weightily tapped this pile with his forefinger. "As your banker," he said, "I must tell you that your family is doing very well. To the extent that it's possible for average people to do so you're all creating nice little estates. This is important, and it becomes increasingly important as your parents near retirement age. And so, for that reason only, understand, I must tell you as your banker that I disapprove this contemplated sale."

"It isn't sensible in a way, I know. It'll probably cost us plenty. But on the other hand, Mr. Callaway, what good is ever accomplished by allowing others to dictate to you."

"I'm certain," he said, and thereby betrayed his interest in supporting the Wakelys, "that no one intended to dictate to you. The worst that the Wakelys can be accused of is fighting for what they think is best for themselves and the community."

"Perhaps that's what I'm doing, too?"

"Another thing," he said quietly. "You're risking something. So are all the others who are supporting Mr. Jackson. In the circumstances isn't it fair to ask what Mr. Jackson is risking?"

"He's been here quite a few weeks, Mr. Callaway, paying his own expenses. He's already spent quite a bit of money looking into land titles, buying information, arranging for supplies and the like."

"All of which items are chargeable to business losses in the event the deal doesn't go through. Which means, in effect, that he isn't out a penny. But you?"

"Well, if the deal doesn't go through I'll have the land still. And as for Dad . . . well, he'll pick up enough work for his crew and truck, and if he doesn't he can operate the motel and live comfortably enough."

"In other words, you refuse to be dissuaded?"

Evalin stood up and looked at her wristwatch. "I think the sooner this phase of it is settled the better it will be for everyone concerned."

He sighed and watched her leave with her head high and her back ramrod straight. And Evalin, driving on, made a mental note to tell Chuck he'd be wrong to depend upon Mr. Callaway's discretion. The bank serviced the mines and the mines' payrolls. Without those accounts there'd probably not be a bank in Thorpe. There it was, another indication of the power and the control the Wakelys exerted in Thorpe. She was surprised that this power and this control had been successfully concealed for so long.

Impulsively she drove to the estate Mr. Wakely had had created in the mountain wilderness. She parked her Morris Minor before the marble steps and went up to the door of Wakely House and gave its bell-button a push. She was answered this time by Mr. Coxe, who'd apparently recovered from the hernia operation he'd had back in early April. But recovery hadn't improved the general condition of his temper. He greeted her with a sour and surly nod. He mumbled "Hello," and that was all, but he did have the grace to lead her up the hall to the library and to announce her visit to Mr. Wakely. After he'd shown her into the old pioneer's presence, he closed the door with a little bang and his footsteps quickly receded down the hall.

Mr. Wakely grinned in his bristly beard. "Coxe wants us to have Jackson arrested. He's cross with me because I'm not inclined to do that."

"Hi, Mr. Wakely."

"Sit down. Nice of you to call. You want my highest bid for that deed and bill-of-sale in your handbag, eh?"

"I thought bankers weren't supposed to discuss confidential business with outsiders."

"They're not, and they don't."

"Well, then, how did you know about the deed and the bill of sale?"

"I'm the bank, Evalin."

She had to laugh. "Every time I see

you, sir, you surprise me."

"That's how you win business scraps. You always have a surprise that carries the day."

"Sometimes," she said, alluding to Bill's surprise one evening in Community Hall, "surprise also costs you the day."

"I intended to tell Bill," he said, sensing her thoughts. "But Bill surprised me by attending that idiotic meeting, by fighting with people who won't ever make the decision anyway."

"It's too bad you didn't tell him, sir."

"About Tom. Tom Meeker isn't an employee. He's a man who works for me under contract. He's in business, in other words. While you might make a good case out of the fact we fired four miners, you can't make a good case for your father. I have the right to hire whatever contractor I want to use to haul my ore to the rolling mill."

"I didn't come here to discuss that, Mr. Wakely."

"You want my price, is that it?"

"No, sir."

His brown eyes flared as Bill's had flared. "Don't fence with me," he warned. "This isn't a game."

"I just thought I should tell you I'm selling to Chuck Jackson."

"You'll wish you hadn't."

"I'm already wishing I didn't have to. Listen, Mr. Wakely, you're not being fair. And you're not being intelligent, either."

He barked short laughter.

"No one intended to battle with you. People wanted a hotel and the resort because it would be good for the town. There's nothing wrong with that."

"I think there is."

"What?"

"It stays as it is. You open it up for this thing and then you'll open it up for something else. It disappears. I didn't find this valley to see it turned into one of those stinking cities that are a stench in the nostrils of humankind. And I didn't open my mines, either, to be told in my old age how and when and why I can operate them. No. Our life here is good. Why, your own savings accounts, your little business, prove I'm not the monster a lot of people now are saying I am. Have I ever interfered before?"

"No."

"Well, there you are. I'm interfering now because I know Jackson's sold you all a bill of fool's gold. I happen to like my town and my people. Yet when I move to protect them, people I thought were my friends turn against me."

"Will you build the hotel and vacation resort?"

"Rubbish. It won't go."

"What happens if the mines close, if the veins peter out?"

"That won't happen."

"Can you guarantee that?"

"No one can guarantee a thing like that."

"Then if it does happen?"

"We all take our chances."

"But it's wrong for us to take a

chance on this hotel and vacation resort?"

His grunt told her she'd scored a point. She nodded, and tried to press her advantage. "You should be fair," she said. "Mr. Wakely, get into this thing with Chuck Jackson. Between the two of you, you could put Thorpe on the map. People would respect you and love you for it. Your interests would be protected and — "

He interrupted harshly: "I run my own show and my own valley. If they want a brawl I'll give them a brawl. I offer you for the land what I've already offered, not a penny more. Either side with me or fight against me; the choice is yours."

"Against."

He came surging up from his chair. "You fool. Don't you know the boy loves you? You could be mistress of Wakely House. Do you know what that means?"

Evalin stood up and took a nervous step backward.

The old man bellowed laughter. He sat down again and gave the desk a blow with his fist. "The nerve of you. You're a rabbit trying to outguess a lion! I ought to smash you to teach you a lesson. If it wasn't for Bill I would."

"That's why I'm against you," Evalin heard herself say. "No one should have that kind of power, Mr. Wakely."

And she hurried from the great mansion to deliver the deed and join the Thorpe Committee for Progress.

13

CHARLES JACKSON was deeply touched. It was, he thought, the finest vote of confidence he'd been given anywhere in the world, and he wanted to wine and dine Evalin Meeker and give her a proper kiss under a Colorado moon. But he did none of these things. Instead, he went over to Montgomery and saw to it that the transfer was properly made and registered. He then chartered an airplane and flew to San Antonio for a weekend of discussions with his father.

His father was delighted to see him. A man as tall as Charles, but much thinner, and his black hair grizzled, Mr. Jackson led his son into the suite of offices he maintained across the road from the Alamo. He sat down behind his glass-topped desk. "Well, to business, if it's business you prefer. How are things in that wilderness Vance discovered?"

"Fine. I have a lot of people behind me, and I have the necessary land."

"Excellent. Was the price pretty steep?"

"Five hundred an acre, and no cash is necessary."

"Indeed?"

Mr. Jackson swung about nervously in his chair and glanced across the street at the historic Alamo. He thought it over for several moments. "A satisfactory deal," he finally said with a show of humor. "I must ask you to teach me the technique."

"It wasn't the technique, sir. It was the girl."

Mr. Jackson turned eagerly. "Are you in love son? How splendid! This will amuse you, I know, but I still have a hankering to dandle a grandson on my knee."

"Of course not, sir!"

"Must you constantly shy off from emotion, son?"

"How could it possibly be love? I just met her a couple of months ago. One kiss. How on earth can you turn that into love?"

"Nothing is finer, son, than love."

"Sure she's attractive. And when you go riding through the hills with her and she talks of the animals and the seasons, you do think that she's a very fine person. But good heavens, sir, I've hardly dated her."

A knock sounded on the pebble-glass door. It was Mr. Jackson's secretary and she was defending, as always, his very tight schedule.

"How do you do, Mr. Charles," she said. "I'm afraid you're running behind schedule, Mr. Jackson."

"Cancel all my appointments, Martha."

Martha laughed in disbelieving tones. "Mr. Charles," she said, "I do wish you wouldn't mix your father up every time you come home. It takes me weeks to get the messes straightened out."

"You see, Martha," Mr. Jackson

smiled, "my son has found himself a girl."

Charles sprang impatiently from his chair. "Will you tell this mawkishly sentimental idiot, Martha, that one kiss, *one*, mind you, doesn't make for romance?"

Mr. Jackson spoke before Martha could. "Martha," he said, "it must have been quite a kiss. Now here's the picture as I see it. Charles, here, was being out-maneuvered, and very beautifully, I must say, by a canny barbarian in the mountains. He needed land. He was blocked from all land but the parcel he wanted and desperately needed. The girl must have been offered a pretty price by the bearded barbarian in the mountains. But Charles kissed her. My son, Martha. This lad before you. And the result? He has the parcel of land, at a ridiculously low cost per acre, and he doesn't even have to pay cash."

Martha chuckled. "Mr. Charles, may I touch you?"

"Hang it all, this is preposterous! It's a bitter fight to Evalin Meeker and — "

"Take that name," snapped Mr. Jackson.

"Her father worked for Wakely. Mind, I use the past tense. Well, when he threatened to fire the father Evalin blew her top."

"Martha?"

"Yes, Mr. Jackson."

"I like her spirit, Martha, don't you?"

"Very, very much, Mr. Jackson. I didn't know people still used the methods Mr. Wakely used, or tried to use."

"So this girl sold the land to me. To her it's a matter of principle. No matter what happens, she said, she's in this fight to stay."

Breathing deeply, Charles again sat down.

"Well, we'll discuss her over the weekend," Mr. Jackson laughed. He dismissed Martha and got a red-beaded pin from a box in his desk. He went over to the large map and found Colorado and stuck the pin into the state southeast of Grand Junction. He stepped backward and looked at the map admiringly.

"A nice addition, I think. Our stockholders will be pleased."

"You're being premature, Dad."

"Do you think so? Why?"

Charles gave him his reasons, a process that used up a good two hours but which left his father with a detailed knowledge of the difficulties still to be dealt with in Thorpe. At the end of this résumé Martha came in again, too insistent to be denied, and Charles went home for lunch and caught his mother swimming in the pool. She gave a squeal of delight when she saw him, and clumsily splashed to the steps and darted up the steps and almost clasped him to her dripping, nicely formed body. But being a practical person, she stopped short of that and just gave him a smacking kiss on the cheek. She led him across the flag-stoned patio and dropped contentedly onto the plastic-strapped chaise-longue. "We'll have a party," she decided. "Everyone has missed you, Pru most of all. She told me just this morning that her tennis hasn't been the same since you left."

"Let's not, Mom."

She had his eyes, a clear dark blue, and she was more sensitive to his moods than his father was. "Well, you sit down and we'll have lunch and we'll talk."

She hailed Catherine, and Catherine trudged out and beamed at Charles and then grimaced in ugly fashion. "Boy," she scolded, "ain't you eatin' your vittles? You want to starve thin?"

Charles grinned and sat down and stared up at the clear Texas sky. He liked the warmth of the day and the sound of bees in the garden and his mother's nearness and even the angry way Catherine swished back to the house to fetch him what she'd think was a proper lunch. It was good to be home, Charles thought, and it was time, he added, that the corporation appointed regional managers to handle such development projects as Thorpe. Men like Vance, who'd seen Thorpe, who'd decided it had possibilities, who'd dug up all the information he'd had to work with in the beginning. Some day, Charles thought, his father would retire and he would have to fill his father's shoes. And since that was so, shouldn't he be learning this end of the business now?

"What's wrong, Charles?" his mother asked.

"Why should anything be wrong?"

"I know, dear. You're a great big man now who can fight a good battle in the business world. But you're also the tot I taught to eat properly and walk and all that. So don't try your pretenses on me. A mother, Charles, has a kind of radar emotional system that goes click-click-click when her son's having emotional difficulties."

He met her wide, unwinking eyes.

He laughed self-consciously. "Oh, it's nothing serious. It's — well, look here, what does a kiss amount to in the long run?"

"Was there a kiss?"

A breeze came along to stir the tropical plants and to wrinkle the green-blue water in the pool. Charles missed something, and then he knew what it was: that his ears were aching for the sounds made by ancient forests in a mountain wind. He grimaced.

"There was a kiss," he admitted. "Nothing behind it, you understand. She was being nonsensical and I wanted to give her a jolt."

Catherine came out with the lunch, and it was a whopper, consisting of several meat sandwiches for Charles, a salad for them both, wedges of cake and a big pitcher of milk. Catherine stood standing in the brilliant sun, her colored face stern, until Charles had swallowed several bites. She then went back to the glass patio door and opened it and stepped inside out of earshot, but stood there where she could watch and provide whatever service was needed.

Noticing, Charles laughed. "You've finally trained her, Mom, haven't you?"

"Catherine? Well, perhaps so. But I think that Catherine has also trained me. She misses you, Chuck. I do, too, and your father does."

"I was just thinking that this ought to be my last field job. I've picked up all the experience I'll need. But there's a great deal about high finance I don't understand, and if I'm to run the works when Dad steps down — "

"I'll talk with him. Is she a nice young lady, Chuck?"

"Very nice."

"Not a butterfly, I hope. I never did like butterflies."

"She works. She runs the motel there."

"I'd like to meet her, I think."

"We haven't dated in the strict sense of the word. Oh, I've gone riding with her a few times, things like that — business to her, of course."

"Or perhaps not."

"No, I'm sure that's it. She's in or thought she was, with the distr attorney there."

"What happened?"

"The district attorney is Wakely's man. He shocked or disillusioned Evalin by more or less betraying that fact to her. Then there's the beautiful doctor from New Jersey, who happens to have a vest-pocket estate, as she calls it, and who's in love with Andrew Pierce, too."

"Such complications!"

"Not really. Pierce is a fellow who had to struggle all his life. Now he's in a position where he thinks he can cash in. He wants to be governor of Colorado. He wants to be rich. So the rest is obvious. If he does Wakely's work Wakely may be able to make him governor — or so Pierce thinks. And if he marries the doctor he could at least have security. He's very logical, this Pierce. To him they aren't complications at all."

his girl they are?"

1 to tell," Charles said
. "I know the battle with
etty much dominates her
ese days. I have concrete
proof of that. But how much of this
battle is for the hotel, and how much
of it is really for Andrew Pierce himself,
is something I can't say."

Mrs. Jackson was proud of her son.
"Now that," she said, "is a point most
people would overlook. The indirect
battle for Andrew Pierce, I mean. But
you could be wrong to think it's that,
and you could be wrong to believe the
few times she went out with you were
business occasions only."

Charles nodded, but he continued to
wonder, and when he returned to the
motel in Thorpe late in the afternoon
of the following Monday, he went
directly to his cabin and stripped down
to his shorts and stretched out on the
comfortable bed to do some thinking
on the subject of Evalin Meeker.

The kiss, he knew, had stirred him

much more deeply than he'd let his parents know.

He got up from the bed. He went to the clothes-closet and took out sport clothes and dressed hurriedly. Anxious to see her, he strode briskly outdoors and up along the path to the big, white-frame house standing beautifully lit by the clean, gold sun . . .

14

EVALIN turned from the stove. She wore lime-green slacks and a white cotton blouse, and she wore a thin, lime-green ribbon in her hair to keep its masses and curls back where they belonged. Her mouth was curved in a smile, but the smile was as cool to the eyes as her costume, and Chuck's warm, happy expression disappeared. This pleased her. And it pleased some perverse streak inside her to say: "Nice to have you back, Chuck. I didn't hear your knock."

He sat down and for a tense moment or so wasn't a brilliant business-man but a very confused and uncertain fellow.

"How was Texas, Chuck?"

"Warm. Pleasant. Interesting. Have you ever been to Texas?"

"No."

"Have you ever been out of this state?"

"No."

"Have you ever even been to Denver?"

"Once." Her brow crinkled prettily. "I didn't like Denver. It's such a huge, crowded city. I like mountains you can get into, not just see, and I like the feel of the mountains around me. To me, Chuck, mountains aren't just dead heaps of stone. I'm like the Indians about mountains. You ask any Indian and he'll tell you the mountains are alive."

"So you like mountains," he smiled, "but aren't you curious about the rest of the world?"

"About people, yes. But not the world."

"No yen ever to see what the rest of the world looks like?"

"Should I have?"

"It's natural."

"It's natural to like your home town, too. Oh, and speaking of that, the support is just rolling in. Mr. Miller tells me the news that you had the land was just the prod people needed. I think they'll put up that money you need."

"I thought I had made it clear that I don't need that money. What I needed was an indication of their support. Words don't matter. A great many words have been spoken since I came to Thorpe. The only important ones were the ones you used to tell me you'd sell me the land."

Evalin turned back to the stove. It was her turn to get the dinner for all the guests in the motel, and she'd not really gotten beyond the beginning stage. But she didn't want to say in so many words that she wanted him to leave. Now that they were in the battle together, she would have to get along with Chuck regardless of the callow way his eyes were studying her so called striking good looks.

"Well," he said, not taking her hint, "it doesn't matter. If the money's brought in, fine. If it isn't, that's fine, too."

About to say more, he closed his mouth, because the door had opened and Dr. Helen Zane had come into the room. The lovely doctor from New Jersey was dressed in shorts and halter and low-cut sneakers. She was breathing hard, as if she'd been playing tennis or something else as strenuous. "Why," she smiled, "its Mr. Jackson. And how was Texas?"

Chuck mumbled something or other about Texas having been all right, and then to Evalin's amusement he left. She grinned at Dr. Zane. "You're back early, aren't you? And I'm afraid I can't talk now, because if I do no one will get dinner."

"It seemed important, Evalin."

"Yes?"

"I stopped for a glass of milk at that Dalton woman's house. Andrew was there, and Bill Wakely was there, and I'm afraid they've decided to be poor sports. As I understand it, people just can't go into business here in willy-nilly fashion. There must be approval by the

County Supervisors, isn't that so?"

"Yes."

"And if the majority were to vote against permitting Charles Jackson to build that hotel, it would stick, wouldn't it?"

"I think so. But of course they wouldn't do that."

"Why not — if doubts can be raised concerning the character of Charles Jackson and the nature of his operations?"

"How could they do that?"

"Did you know, for instance, that his corporation doesn't own any of the hotels or motels or businesses it operates?"

Evalin whirled.

The glossy black head snapped back, and Dr. Zane added dryly: "I see that you didn't."

"But that's ridiculous!"

"It's too involved for me, frankly. But as I understand it, the corporation is a management corporation that seldom invests much of its own capital. Once it has acquired land and made its surveys, it obtains the necessary financing from banks and other leading institutions. Those are long-term things, according to Andrew Pierce, and the corporation's income is the percentage of the profits it receives for managing the thing. Another thing that Andrew discovered is this: that actually the Jacksons own very little of the corporation, either. They're paid a whopping income to run the corporation, and that's all."

Evalin decided it was all too involved for her, too. "What difference does it make?" she asked. "The hotel will be built and operated and we'll prosper, won't we?"

"Not," said Dr. Helen Zane, "if Mr. Wakely can convince a majority of the supervisors that the Jacksons are people who are speculating with someone else's money. The question then, you see, is whether this will be a legitimate interest that will benefit the area, or whether it will be just another speculator's football. If he can convince them of the latter, they'll hardly oppose a man who is operating an established and profitable business here, will they?"

"They're elected by the people. They'll vote as the people want them to vote."

"But if the Jacksons are discredited?"

Intuition told Evalin at that point that Dr. Helen Zane wasn't posing hypothetical questions, that she was actually telling her the course of action that Andrew had mapped out and that the Wakelys would back to the limit.

She said impulsively: "If that's tried, Dr. Zane, your Andrew Pierce will have to come out into the open. If they won, his position here in the county would be solid. If he lost I'm afraid he'd lose his job."

"I know."

"Well, then . . . "

"I might prefer it that way. Andrew's all right. I believe that, and I'll work for him as I can. He just got off on the wrong foot, and getting the backing of Wakely didn't help Andrew's character, not by a jugful. In a different state, in a proper law office, with the proper backing and connections . . . "

"I don't know." Evalin shook her head. "Things go so strangely, Dr. Zane. Back in April I expected to be proposed to one lovely afternoon. Now here it is almost the end of July and everything's so mixed up for me. Anyway, I'd better get dinner."

"I'd like you to let the thing run its course."

"Why?"

"It would be better for Andrew if he lost."

"What could I do to prevent it?"

"Tell Charles Jackson what I've just told you."

"But — "

"And you want the truth about him, too, don't you? How could you get that if he were warned, given time to prepare?"

Evalin had to laugh. "But he

knows already, Dr. Zane. He's buying information from Lenore Dalton, didn't you know?"

Dr. Helen Zane groaned. "Then there won't be a battle after all? What a shame."

She left, gloomy-faced, and Evalin cooked the dinner and freshened up and then served the dinner and took part in the small-talk in the papered dining-room left of the long, broad hall. After dinner she went out back to the stables and found Bert studying as usual in the tack-room, but this time pleased to have her company. He actually got up and dusted a chair and saw to it that she was seated comfortably. Then he turned off the goose-neck desk-lamp and sat down, tilting the chair back to rest against the board-and-batten wall.

"I got an offer for a job, Miss Evalin."

"Oh?"

"Bill Wakely. He called me over in town the other day and asked me if I thought I could do payroll checking, things like that."

"Really?"

The thin face was bright with excitement; there was more sparkle in the boy's brown eyes than there'd been in months. "I could do that job, Miss Evalin. I'm pretty good at maths, and the way I figure it, I'll have more time for studying and a chance to get some rest, too."

"But I thought you once told me you wouldn't work for the Wakelys because you didn't want to live so far from town."

"This would be at headquarters," he explained. "I could live out back, too, Bill Wakely said, and rent free if I keep the place cleaned up."

Evalin loosed a low, soft whistle. "That's pretty good, Bert. I hope you told him you'd accept?"

The front legs of the chair came down hard. Bert said stiffly: "I don't leave in the lurch folks who've been nice to me. I give them notice before

I quit. Before I give notice I talk things over with them."

"But I think you know by now, Bert, that my mother and dad want you to get ahead. And I do, too. So we wouldn't stand in your way. What about August first? By that time some of the guests will be moving on, and if I do need a fellow out here I'll be able to pick one up in town. Perhaps one of those men the Wakelys fired, I don't know."

"He's upset, Miss Evalin."

"Who is?"

"Bill Wakely."

"Well, I should think he would be! I'm ashamed of him! He isn't this way at all, and he knows it, and he knows that I know it, and if he had the gumption he was born with he'd do the right thing for everyone concerned."

Bert's brown eyes danced. "That's the girl, Miss Evalin; give him what for."

Evalin got to her feet. "Be seventeen,"

she said; "just be your age, little boy, will you?"

"He'd like to see you, Miss Evalin."

She turned and studied Bert's thin, freckled face. "Did he say so?"

"He said so."

"Well, will you give him a message for me? Will you tell Bill I'll go picknicking with him the day he behaves like the Bill I used to know and respect?"

"Sure."

"But that I won't see him until he does behave the way he knows that he should behave?"

"Aw . . . "

"I mean that."

She went restlessly back to the house. But it was too warm and stuffy there, and she decided to take a walk. She got a sweater from her room and left by way of the front door and followed the west parking area to its junction with the drive. As she neared the stone gateposts she heard steps behind her and she barely suppressed a rising chuckle. She stopped and put her sweater on and methodically buttoned it. Then, her hands in its pockets, she ambled on to the creek splashing along its ancient course toward its pre-destined meeting with Thorpe River. She sat down on a bench under one of the trees and watched the sparkling water. When Chuck self-consciously joined her on the bench, she looked up and gently smiled.

"It's lovely, Chuck, isn't it?"

"Very."

"The nice thing about the mountains, Chuck, is that you can find in them beauty to suit your every mood. If you're feeling in a stern mood there are the stern peaks with their caps of snow. If spring's in your heart there are — "

She broke off, having noticed the little slide he'd made on the bench in her direction.

"Is spring in your heart?" she asked bluntly.

"Evalin . . . "

"Chuck, I did sell you that land

because I wanted to see progress come to Thorpe. There was no other reason."

"Evalin . . . "

"I know, Chuck. You have looked upon my fair face with its dimples and ruby lips and you have decided it's beauteous and worth kissing. And there's the moon and our silver, romantic mountains, and the lonely summer guest and the propinquity of that fair and beauteous face. It's such an old, old story, Chuck."

She noticed that he'd attained another six inches while she'd been talking.

She stood up, politely covered a yawn. "Well, I'd better get back indoors."

"What are you afraid of, Evalin?"

She didn't know. She knew that she'd felt drawn toward him even before she'd been kissed. And she supposed that after the kiss she'd felt more strongly drawn toward him than before, but beyond that she knew nothing except that she didn't want any more nonsense. Was that it? Was she afraid there'd be more nonsense?

"I know," Chuck Jackson said, "it isn't logical. We've gone riding a few times, we've never sat down for a serious talk with one another. Still . . . "

"No, Chuck."

Her voice was so cold it did stop him in the act of reaching out for her.

He said gruffly: "As you wish. I can understand how you feel because I felt that same way. Later, when all this is over, perhaps there'll be more time for talking and even logic. I'll be here for many, many months, Evalin. This will be my last field job. I've settled that with my father. So I'll want to make sure it's the best of the lot. Or so, at least, I told my mother."

"I see."

"I'd like to date you, Evalin. I'd like that very much."

"Listen, Chuck — "

"It isn't Pierce, because Pierce is in love with the doctor and you know it. I want to apologize, by the way, for the things I said about that one night. It was natural and normal for you to be civilized. You knew it was over, and so — "

"I didn't! Not then!"

"And I ought to apologize for the kiss, I think. It should have been tender. Don't you think love should be tender?"

"Chuck, I — "

"And it isn't Bill Wakely, Evalin. You can't love a cheat. In fact — "

He jumped backward, but not in time. Her hand, a white blur in the moonlight, cracked against his cheek. And Evalin, storming forward, began to shrill: "You take that back! You take that back!"

He didn't. All he said, before leaving, was something to the effect that all men appreciated loyalty. And then he was gone, leaving Evalin's mind in confusion and her heartbeats jerky and heavy.

Why did they always talk of love? she wondered.

15

THE attack came, and it was savagely made by the old pioneer himself. He made a speech in Community Hall, and the fact that most of his audience was there because it was afraid not to be there didn't inhibit him a bit. Evalin heard herself denounced as a muddle-headed, emotional fool who'd betrayed her home town and her so-called friends for the stars in a handsome man's eyes. She heard Charles Jackson denounced as a clever, big-city slicker who worked with other people's money and other people's land to enrich his father and himself. She heard, finally, a demand that a meeting of the County Supervisors be called to settle the question once and for all. And then came the bombshell. If this meeting weren't promptly called the mines would be closed down utterly. "I'm sick and tired," came the roar, "of being accused of cold-bloodedly and deliberately trying to freeze other business out so that I can get away with paying starvation wages. The truth is that I've been opposed to this sharpshooter from the very beginning because I knew from the beginning that he was a sharpshooter. Now we'll bring it out into the open, and so that no one can claim I'm in this for profit, I won't mine a gram of gold until this business is finally decided."

You could all but hear the proverbial pin drop as he turned and strode from the stage.

That troubled Evalin.

She quickly sprang to her feet.

"Mr. Wakely," she called, "one moment, please."

The old man spun. The old brown eyes glared. "Well?"

"I intend to sue you for slander," Evalin said.

He smashed back: "Sue your

muddle-headed head off."

Evalin left the meeting. Now people were buzzing excitedly and the buzzes told her she'd accomplished her purpose. The show of spirit had encouraged others, and as the buzzes became hoots and catcalls of derision she burst into laughter. She drove home and changed into riding clothes and had Bert saddle up Mighty Hunter. She gave the mighty bay his head, and as he trotted off across the escarpment of scrub oak and brush due west, she thrust the whole unpleasantness involving Mr. Wakely and Bill and Andrew from her mind. She'd ride all the way up to Sheep Meadow, she decided, in the shadow of great Angel Mountain. It had been too long since she'd done that. The truth was that she'd become too emotionally involved, really, in a business matter that didn't concern her. She'd done her part. Now let others do theirs.

A quarter-mile beyond the escarpment the trail curved south from the road. It carried over a flashing stream to a gentle slope, and at the summit was a flatland colorful with shrubs and flowers. The air hummed with the sound of bees. Birds were everywhere to be seen, sounding their songs in a pretty way that made her think of shepherd's pipes and then of the sheep she'd seen marching through town one day en route to the summer range. She wondered where those sheep were now. She glanced up among the towering mountains and saw trees, then multicolored stone above timber-line, then rimrock, then an eagle or two, but nothing that resembled sheep.

She jerked Mighty Hunter to a halt, struck by a sudden vista of alpine gold-flowers. For as far as her eye could see the carpet of vivid yellow stretched, rolling down into gullies, rolling up the slopes toward the tundras of the highest peaks. She spotted a groundhog scurrying along, a bright cinnamon brown. Far ahead in one of the meadows she spotted elk, and she was amused to notice that not even shouting at them could frighten them from the sweet mountain-grass.

As they went on there was an incident.

They flushed a deer, and the deer whirled and charged off with springy bounds, and Mighty Hunter seemed to deem that a challenge. Instantly the great bay surged forward, leaping a fallen tree, crashing through mountain laurel and cinquefoil, Indian paintbrush and tangles of ivy. He hurled a mighty scream of defiance at the forest world, and at once the forest world cried back, Rocky Mountain jays squawking, magpies chattering, squirrels scolding and a bear, no less, coughing hollow-voiced irritation.

Evalin gasped.

Just in time she dug her knees in and gripped the saddle-horn hard. Mighty Hunter's sudden stop sent him skidding through the humus and underbrush to his knees, and only a final last-second fling of her arms around his neck saved Evalin a very nasty throw. She dismounted hurriedly, so disgusted her nose quivered with scorn. "Oh, fine," she scolded. "Behold the big brave horse. It was just a bear, you goop. He was probably more afraid than you were."

Mighty Hunter stood up and shook himself. He glanced left with rolling eyes. And then, quite as though he feared nothing that walked or growled or even wriggled, he dropped his head to nip at the brownish-green remains of wild crocus. He ambled off. Having been insulted, he refused to obey her call. He pushed on ten or fifteen feet and, his tail swishing, his head high, he gazed off through the tremulous aspen leaves at a distant patch of turquoise sky.

Evalin sat down to wait.

When she grew tired of that she rose and stretched and thrust her Stetson back and her head and ambled through the grove to the trail she knew would carry her to Camp Travis Mine. It was a pleasant walk. The trail broadened to become an ore road, really, and the road swung outward to the cliff and gave her a magnificent view of Lost River Gorge. She enjoyed the falls several minutes and then, hearing a truck lumbering up the road, she turned to bum a ride.

Meeting Bill's astonished gaze, she changed her mind.

Bill stopped the truck anyway. "You're trespassing, Ev. This land's posted, you know that."

She grinned and brushed dust from her levis. She studied the big ore truck. She wondered what Bill was doing with it in that end of the property. There was nothing there except forest and rocks and gorges.

"Well, hop in," he said. "I'll take you down to the sheriff."

"No, thanks."

"I'm serious, Ev. This is gold mine country. We trust our friends; we don't trust our announced enemies. I'm sorry, but that's how it has to be."

"I was thrown. And you know who

did it, too. You gave me Mighty Hunter. And you didn't train him properly, because every time he hears a bear he goes panicky."

Bill's lips twitched. When he finally smiled his teeth were very white against the deep tan of his face. "Oh, I see. And I suppose I gave him to you, Ev, in the big hope he'd break your neck some day?"

"I wouldn't put it past you! To think we were friends! I'm ashamed of myself."

"Look, there's a lot you don't know."

"Such as? And don't tell me lies, either."

He grimaced. But Mighty Hunter, having heard voices, and perhaps thinking he'd be abandoned, came loping over to Evalin and nuzzled her.

Evalin jumped into the saddle. Looking down at Bill, she challenged: "Well?"

"Now listen to me, Evalin. You

237

never gave us the — "

"Bill, where on earth did you get that gold ore?"

"It's tailings, you fool. Now will you listen?"

She laughed jeeringly. "Oh, sure. My Dad's hauled ore for you people for years and so, of course, I don't know the difference between ore and tailings. What did you do, open up the rear end of the mine at last?"

"I could shoot you, Evalin, just like that. This is posted property and you're here without my permission. So will you listen to me?"

"Well?"

"You see tailings, Ev, is that understood?"

A cold breeze, more fancied than real, swirled about Evalin's head. She looked at Bill's tight, hard face, and inexplicably she shivered.

"Go on, Bill."

He got out of the truck. He seemed reluctant to talk now that he had her complete attention. And he didn't seem to be himself as he got a rock and placed it in the middle of the ore-road and sat down on it. His steps had no spring. His shoulders were slumped, his head dropped a bit as if he were physically worn out.

"Are you all right, Bill?"

"Why shouldn't I be?"

She stared at his shoes. They were muddy up almost to their tops. "You've been working hard a long time, Bill, I should judge. I missed you at the meeting. Apparently you were too busy working up here to attend the meeting. Working up here alone, too, I think. Bill?"

"Well?"

"I'm very fond of you, Bill."

"Sure, Ev, sure."

Evalin got down from Mighty Hunter. She felt oddly weary herself, as if some of the tension that had existed in Thorpe ever since the battle had begun had somehow gotten inside her to punish her nerves and muscles and mind. Now that it was over, now that she understood too many things, and Bill most of all, she wanted to lie down somewhere and cry herself to sleep.

"I am, Bill. If I'd had a brother I'd have wanted him to be like you. That's love, Bill, and perhaps it's the finest love of all, because there's no asking in it, none of the asking that's in even the relationship of a wife with her husband. Please, Bill, do you understand that — "

He raised his eyes. He was ashen now, and his lips were trembling. When he asked: "What do you know?" his voice was husky and unrecognizable as his own.

"I don't doubt there are tailings down there, Bill. But under the tailings there's gold ore. Am I right?"

"No."

"Don't lie."

"I said no."

"Bill, one word from me and it could be proved or disproved just like that."

He shook his head as if to clear it of weariness and confusion.

"And that explains the mystery, Bill, doesn't it? Ah, what a clever man your Gramps is. See how beautifully he led us astray. Bill, he's a great actor, isn't he? One day he raged so at me I thought he'd lost his sense. I can still hear him bellowing that before he's dragged down he'll draw blood. And I thought, as he wanted me to think, that it was all tied up with a queer lust for power and control."

Bill said nothing. He began to cough, as a man will if he works too long with shovel and pick in thin mountain air.

Evalin hurried to him. She knelt beside him on the ore-road and she took her tiny bottle of smelling salts from her levis. She opened the bottle, thrust it under Bill's nose. "Inhale," she smiled. "And don't think it's sissy, Bill. It does help; that's why I carry this bottle. Recognize this bottle, by the way? You gave it to me when I was twelve and you were fourteen because you'd read in some silly book that weak females were always fainting and needed a bottle of smelling-salts handy."

He inhaled.

She continued as it came to her clearly at last. "And of course your grandfather didn't offer me too high a price for the land because if he had it would have made me suspicious. Is that so?"

"Andrew suggested that possibility."

"Andrew was involved?"

He nodded. "Why do you think I was always against him? I didn't know about this. I did know about a few other things."

"What did Mr. Wakely do, Bill — mine over his quota?"

"Yes. He apparently thought he could get above the announced market price. I don't know the whole deal. But when there's unrest around the world people with money want gold. Gold is marketable anywhere. Currency can be cheapened or even downed. Down at the meeting, did Gramps say we were closing for a while?"

"Yes."

"I did that. I found out about all this a couple of months ago, Evalin. Some fellows were snooping, and I fired them, and I did some snooping on my own."

"The men who spoke up at the meeting? Bill — " Then Evalin saw that couldn't be. The time angle was wrong.

"Since then," he said with a forced grin, "I've been a pretty busy guy. When I got things lined up I sprang it on Gramps."

"And the meeting of the County Supervisors is really an effort to gain time?"

"Yes."

"But if this is the last load, Bill — "

"How do I know I won't find more?"

"I see."

"Ev?"

"Bill?"

"You didn't see anything, Ev."

She got up and walked back to Mighty Hunter, and she climbed onto the saddle and gazed off at Angel Mountain standing huge and lovely against the sky. She recalled that her first trip way up almost to the top had been made with Bill and her father. She recalled that Bill had been involved in so many of her firsts, and that of all the people she'd known Bill had been the most dependable and loyal. Until, of course, his loyalty to an old pirate had come between them. And how could she say that in similar circumstances she'd not have done what Bill had done?

"Well, Ev?"

"I saw nothing, Bill."

16

APPROPRIATELY, it stormed. Huge, greenish-black clouds struck down from the northwest and blotted out the mountains and forests and seemed to shrink the world. A mutter of thunder sounded behind Angel Mountain, and this mutter was echoed and reechoed, rattling among the peaks and in the assorted gorges.

Evalin hurried downstairs to make certain the windows were closed, and then she got into her raincoat and dashed outdoors for a check-up of the cabins. She loved the cool, damp wind on her face and in her hair. The excitement in the storm stirred her, and she had the nonsensical urge to saddle up Mighty Hunter and go riding up to the mountains to its very core. But the Denbys called her from cabin 1 and she had to go inside and close a balky window.

She discovered that Mr. Denby was excited, too.

"Love 'em!" he said. "Always did, always will."

Mrs. Denby moaned. "I do hope," she said, "that it won't be one of your howlers."

Evalin hurried on. The other guests had closed their windows, and most of them were getting ready to go to the great frame house to sit the storm out. But not Chuck. He came to the door in answer to her knock, and his grin was very broad and happy. "Ready? Well, it'll just take me a minute to freshen up. I've worked out the details of the stupid settlement. I'm not happy about the whole thing, but if you can swing it I suppose it had better have everything you want in it."

"I can swing it, Chuck. And as I've told you before, the five hundred an acre will be profit enough for me. The land only cost Dad ten dollars an acre. For years we've gotten grazing fees out of it. So the five hundred an acre will really be net, and ten thousand in cash — well, we're not pigs."

"You could demand a percentage of the profits."

"And everyone else could, and then how would the hotel make money? If it didn't make money it would be closed in a couple of years. Anyway, don't you realize we'll make money, too? Not all the people who'll want to come to Thorpe will be able to afford your rates. So our motel will prosper, and there you are."

"In business, Evalin, you don't think about things like that. You think of the extra profits you can make."

She smiled wryly, reflecting that it had been just such thinking on the part of old Silas P. Wakely that had gotten him into this difficulty. The extra profit wasn't always profit in the end. Sometimes it could be very, very costly.

"I'll be back," she said. "But I think

we should wait until this storm's over, don't you?"

"No." And now his manner became crisp, aggressive. His deep blue eyes flashed. "I've wasted too much time on this deal. Now that we can settle the question I want to get it settled. After that you and I are going to see a great deal of one another."

Evalin flushed and hurried on toward the creek. She heard the creek roaring along, and as she swung into the wind she discovered that the wind had strengthened and that the raindrops were smaller and colder than they'd been just a few minutes before. The last few steps it took her to reach Dr. Zane's cabin were difficult steps. She was panting and dripping wet, and her hair had been blown in all directions by the time she reached the shelter of the little porch. Dr. Zane opened up quickly to her knock and clucked maternally. "That's a good way to kill yourself, Evalin. You'll either be blown to smithereens or struck by lightning or be felled by a dreadful germ. Come on in."

"Sorry, Dr. Zane; I have an appointment with the Wakelys. Everything here all right?"

"I'm coming with you."

"Nope."

"I have that right."

"Nope."

"Listen," and now the doctor's gray eyes were cold and grim, "I don't care what Andrew has done or tried to do. I love him and I want to be there for the aftermath."

"Nope."

Dr. Zane stepped back from the door, and Evalin went into the little vestibule. Rain water trickling from her coat and stormshoes formed little puddles on the linoleum floor, but she didn't notice that, nor did Dr. Zane. Thunder roared as Evalin closed the door behind her, and Dr. Zane smiled tautly. "A fine day," she said, "for smashing a man's career."

"Andrew did that to himself."

"I'm not complaining. I told you what I hoped would happen. I'm just mentioning that it's a fine day for a nasty, painful business."

"What can I do? The whole thing was ugly from beginning to end. There was never a legitimate reason for opposing Chuck's plans. I told you once that we need more than just one business here in Thorpe. The fact that others who worked for Mr. Wakely risked their jobs and security to help Chuck should prove to you how real that need is. Now that we have the beginning in our grasp we can't let go. I'm not feeling vengeful, Dr. Zane. I thought back in April that it was love. Sure, I daydreamed and I even made practical plans. But it didn't work out, and you never heard one complaint from me. Now that his daydreams won't work out for him either, Andrew has no right to complain. Nor you."

"What have you got?"

"Enough, Dr. Zane, to smash his career in Colorado."

"Why couldn't he just resign? You know what I'm thinking about, of course. He may want a political career in New Jersey. A scandal here — well, why couldn't he just resign?"

It was, Evalin thought, the easy way out. Only if Andrew got away with it, what guarantees did she or even Dr. Zane have that he wouldn't try the same tactics elsewhere? He'd not done much harm in Thorpe — he'd lacked the time. But say that in New Jersey he had the necessary time? The result would be what?

She shook her head.

The lovely doctor from New Jersey frowned. "That's it?"

"It has to be."

"You can be stubborn, can't you? Once you made up your mind to support Charles Jackson you — well, never mind. I'll be leaving tomorrow, Evalin. So far as I'm concerned the summer's over, and I must say I didn't enjoy your Colorado summer very much."

"I'm sorry. He's all right, Helen. I mean, Andrew had such a struggle you can't blame him for wanting to take one shortcut to success. The temptation must have been very great. I'm not sure I'd not have succumbed to such a temptation myself. I think that when you consider all that — well, he's all right."

Amazingly, Dr. Helen Zane laughed derisively. "He's not, and you know it. He's greedy and too ambitious, and he'll junk anyone who isn't useful to him, exactly the way he junked you. But he loves me in his way, and I love him, and I'll be useful to him and it will work out. Are you sure I can't go with you?"

"It would be better if you didn't. But why don't you get in touch with him say this evening?"

"Will he require a doctor, do you think?"

"And a doctor's love, Helen. I think he'll require that most of all."

Helen Zane inhaled deeply, and as

she left Evalin took with her a memory of a face of pain. And when she faced Andrew and Silas P. Wakely and Bill in the library of Wakely House an hour later she was thinking about that face of pain and was pitying Helen because she herself had known not too long ago exactly what that pain was. You believed; then there was nothing to believe. You hoped; then the hope was dashed. You continued to love, in a sense, but even that hurt bitterly, because a segment of your mind was acutely aware that what you loved wasn't really worth loving.

She sighed and switched her gaze from Andrew to the window and the rain sluicing down outside. There in the library the sounds of the storm were faint and she supposed that the storm was petering out. She hoped so. Storms always made the guests restless. With guests underfoot in the frame house, it was very difficult for the Meekers to live their own lives. She hoped the storm was disappearing, because when this was over she wanted to stretch out on her bed early and do some thinking.

Chuck's voice recalled her tense, wandering mind. She glanced back at the men and discovered that the amenities had been taken care of, that Chuck and Andrew were puffing on cigars, that Bill had sat down, that the old man with the bristling beard and the savage brown eyes had in effect called the meeting to order. He was saying, undaunted:

"Pierce here is my legal adviser, Jackson. We concede nothing, we offer nothing except the original five thousand you turned down. Let's begin from there."

Bill spoke, his ruggedly handsome face tight and hard with tension, but still affectionate. "To begin with, Gramps, they know about the gold. Evalin caught me with the last of the stuff."

Mr. Wakely's expression never changed. "Did you say the last of the stuff, Bill?"

"That's it, Gramps."

"Then what do they have in their rifles? Ammunition that can kill? No? The cartridges are blanks, then? Of course?"

Evalin thought she should add her two cents worth. "It would be questionable," she said, "if Andrew or any other lawyer could discredit me, Mr. Wakely. And I very much doubt that Bill in a court of law could say that I lied. Bill and I are very old and very good friends. He loves you very deeply, of course, but I don't think Bill could lie convincingly even to protect you."

The brown eyes darted to her face. "I could buy your motel for fifty thousand in cash. Or I could establish a trust fund that would take care of your parents in their old age."

"But say," she continued, ignoring the offered bribe, "that Bill could and did lie convincingly. You know miners, Mr. Wakely. They get around a territory. They see things. Don't you think that if the accusation were made, there'd be men who'd remember certain things and that all these things, put together, would tend to support my story?"

"No," Andrew answered. His hazel eyes flicked to Evalin's face. There was no emotion in them. If he'd ever loved her, the love was gone, and this was greed and ambition talking, and perhaps fear, as well. "I could make a shambles of such testimony."

"But I wouldn't lie," Bill said. "The other day Ev and I made an agreement. The gold's where it belongs. It'll become part of our quota, and no crime is committed, and no crime was committed since none of the gold was sold illegally. We're back to where we were before it was mined and hidden under that pile of tailings. Only with this difference, Gramps. You and Chuck Jackson here make peace, and Andrew get his head chopped off."

The old man roared: "You had

no right to make any arrangements with her."

"I made them, Gramps. We'll honor them."

"You young pup, don't you dictate to me. Do you know who I am? I discovered this valley. I discovered the gold, and it's my gold to do with as I darned well please."

"No, Gramps."

Quietly spoken, it was nevertheless effective. Dumbfounded by this show of resistance, Mr. Wakely, for the first time, lost his aplomb.

Brawny Bill stood up, and Evalin had never been prouder or fonder of him. His hands on his hips, his tow head high, he met his grandfather's gaze foursquare. "You know how I am, sir. I've stuck all these years and I'll go on sticking. It don't matter about the farm any more. I guess if I'd wanted that I'd have fought for it, the way I'm fighting now. But you don't start a battle now you can't win. You don't disgrace yourself or me. You've got all the money you'll ever need, and I won't stand for you continuing this battle just for reasons of pride."

Andrew stood up, too. He said flatly: "My head won't be chopped off, Bill."

"You're through, Andrew. That's part of the settlement."

"Not after all the dirty work I've done for Mr. Wakely, Bill. We had an agreement and he'll stick to it."

It was the wrong approach. Quickly the head with its shaggy gray hair and its bristling beard swung around. "You shut up," Mr. Wakely ordered. "You were playing for high stakes. It was a gamble, and if you've lost then you've lost, and there isn't a darned thing you can do."

"That's unfair."

"You bet it's unfair. But since when have you worried about fair play?"

Andrew took an angry step forward. Then he changed his mind and spun to quiet Charles Jackson. "Listen, do you want to know how to become top dog in this valley? I can show you how. I can show you things about this valley you never knew and never will know."

Evalin, at that point, began to feel nauseated.

Chuck ignored him. He looked beyond the tense, panicky Andrew and grinned at Silas P. Wakely. "I think," he said, "that you have no choice, sir. And here's another thing. There's no reason to fight now. The ore is gone; no one will discover anything if he should happen to wander onto your property. As for the rest, no one intends to interfere with your operations. Actually, they'll have a fine tourists' value, and my people would encourage you to continue them; they certainly wouldn't try to limit you."

Silas P. Wakely scowled.

Bill shrugged. "It'll be that way, Jackson. It'll take him some time to come around, but he'll come around all right."

"I did nothing illegal!"

Evalin smiled, recognizing the

259

beginning of the end.

"No sir, you did nothing illegal."

"I was holding that gold ore for a rise in price, that was all. And I never lied about my quota. You can check my books."

Andrew turned. "And I get the dirty end of the stick? I did everything you asked me to, and I get the dirty end of the stick?"

Evalin couldn't even feel sorry for him.

17

FOR the guests, the following week, the story was interesting reading. They discussed it at the dinner tables, and it was the opinion of some that there was more in the story than met the eye. Old Mr. Linden put that opinion into words. Looking sharply at Evalin's face, he snapped: "Can't tell me the old boy surrendered easily. Nonsense. You caught him at something, ten to one."

Evalin looked down at her plate. She said nothing because there was nothing to say.

She discovered, next day, that others in Thorpe shared Mr. Linden's suspicion. In the grocery store Mr. Gifford was expounding on this same theme to the group of men sitting huddled about the stove at the rear. "What I think," Mr. Gifford was saying, "is that Wakely was up to something and that they scotched him. It don't stand to reason, now does it, that a business-man like Wakely was opposed all along just because he wanted power? Nope, it doesn't. He had some other reason and — "

He broke off, seeing Evalin. He bustled over and admired the pretty sight she made in her wool plaid skirt and her brown cashmere sweater. "Guess you're pretty rich now, Evalin, huh?"

"Ten thousand dollars richer, Mr. Gifford, as I'm sure you know."

"We'll all be richer, starting next year. It stands to reason. Well, you got your list handy?"

Evalin gave him the list.

Mr. Gifford whistled. "Ain't there some mistake? What with folks leaving pretty soon and — "

"More are coming, Mr. Gifford. Chuck's working pretty fast. Next week quite a crew will be flying in to look over the terrain. And they've even gotten a forecast of the weather for the next five or six weeks. They think they'll get a lot of work done — the property cleared, at least — before the snow flies."

"Whew!"

"I'll pick the things up later, Mr. Gifford; all right?"

"I could deliver them."

"Not necessary."

Evalin went outdoors and drove over to Lenore's place. She went into the wretched house and wasn't surprised to find the dining-room empty and Lenore just puttering about her small kitchen. She studied the redhead's face. "Business fallen off?"

"Doesn't it always, honey?"

"What about working for me?"

"Huh?"

"We'll do a rush business, Lenore. And when the bad weather comes no one will want to drive down here to you for his meals. So why don't you come work for us? Bert's leaving, and you could have his quarters out back.

They're very comfortable, really. You could have your child with you, and next year, of course, Chuck will give you that job he promised you."

The green eyes rounded. "He told you that?"

"Yes."

"It wasn't spying. It was up to Andrew Pierce and the others to watch their tongues."

"It was spying. But as you say, they should have known better than to do their talking in public. What a strange person Andrew is. He never seemed to think people might resent being used."

"I sure feel sorry for that doctor."

"Oh?"

"Andrew came here last week looking mad enough to commit murder. You should've heard him sound off. Boy, there's a guy with a rotten temper! If you ever thought he loved you, honey, just forget it. He didn't. He blamed you for it all, and did he fry you!"

Evalin could imagine the scene.

She said honestly: "I did think back in April that he loved me."

"You're lucky, honey. You know, I got a theory about things. I got the theory that if you try to play things straight, things pretty much work out for the best. Like I always gave my customers value for their dough, so you're offering me this job that I'll take. Well, it was that way with you. You was ready to marry the lug, and that wouldn't have been good, so along came that Vance and then Mr. Jackson and all this fuss and a lot of pressure that made Andrew show what he really was. So now he's gone and maybe you've grown up some and — hey, want some coffee?"

Bill came in, and it wasn't coincidence. He grinned and said: "I've been looking for you. How about a cup of coffee on me?"

It was like old times to Evalin. She nodded eagerly, and they went out into the cold empty dining-room, and Lenore served them coffee and then withdrew discreetly into the kitchen and ostentatiously closed the door behind her.

Bill saucered his coffee to cool it.

Evalin frowned.

Bill poured the coffee back into his cup. "Sorry."

"You should be."

"You forget manners sometimes. Up at the mines the big thing is get the coffee drinkable in a hurry."

"You're a barbarian."

"Sure." He threw his head back and laughed.

"But," she conceded, "a pretty nice and honest one. Bill, I was proud of you at your house. That bearded scoundrel was right. That's what Chuck told me. If you'd not kept your agreement we'd all still be scrapping."

"You kept yours."

"Still — "

"Sure, I'm a swell guy," he jeered. "But you won't marry me?"

"Bill . . . "

"I could give you a life. Look, things

are different with me and Gramps now. Other day Gramps called me into the library. He said he's getting old. Him! He said maybe it was time I took it all over, and did I want to. He don't blame me for what happened. I thought he'd chew my head off. But, instead, he thanked me for trying to keep him out of jail."

"You did, Bill."

"Ah, you were running a bluff."

Evalin shook her head. "No. I was angry enough to have reported him. He was cruel and dishonest and shameful. I would have reported him, believe me."

Meeting her blazing blue eyes, he did believe her, and winced.

"Yeah, I guess you would've. You're a funny girl, Ev. You can be so sweet and then you can turn real rugged. I guess you're the mountains, huh?"

"I guess so."

He sipped his coffee. He lit a cigarette. He then reached into his pocket and took out a plush box

267

and opened the box and produced a diamond engagement ring. The stone was large, a good carat at the very least. The stone glittered with a rich blue fire.

"Want this, Ev?"

"Listen, Bill — "

"I know. But take it another way, Ev. We know one another. We get along fine. I've got enough love for two, and I can give you things. One thing's for sure. Since we'd own most of these mountains, you'd have the mountains as long as you lived."

She glanced down at her cup. She remembered she'd not sugared her coffee and she did so.

"A fellow like Chuck, Ev, he's all right. But what's his life? He goes here, he goes there, and maybe all that means as much to him as the mountains do to you. And maybe it's a fussed-up life at that. Maybe when all's said and done, you'd be lots happier with me."

She raised her eyes, and they were

the grinning, dancing eyes of old. "I didn't know, you see, that I was in love with Mr. Jackson. Thanks for telling me, Bill."

"Aw, it sticks out all over you."

"Does it? Strange. I don't know the man, hardly. Am I such a romantic as all that?"

Bill shrugged, took back the ring. "Well, that's my offer, Ev."

She realized it wasn't a joking matter and she quickly reached out and gripped his hand. "You goof, don't you think I'd say yes if I could? But it wouldn't work, Bill. You'd be cheated, for one thing. For another, it wouldn't make sense without love. Look at my folks. That's what you want and that's what I want, isn't it?"

"Just the same — "

She rose quickly, realizing that was the only way to settle it. "I'd better get back to the motel, Bill. By the way, would you mind helping Lenore move up to the motel? She'll be working for us until the hotel's built."

"Sure."

"And congratulations, Bill, about the mines, I mean. Perhaps Mr. Wakely was right about the farming after all."

"The trouble with Gramps," said Bill, "is that he's been living in the past. In the past his methods worked; there wasn't any law to speak of and you could do what you pleased. Gramps just never mellowed with the times, that's all."

"He's an old pirate! And if he thinks he'll get a Christmas fruitcake from the Meekers this year he'll be disappointed, believe me."

"Wanna bet?"

She met his twinkling brown eyes. She made a face at him and went back to her car. She picked up her groceries at the store and then, all business attended to, drove back toward the motel high on its plateau on the outskirts of Thorpe.

She braked her car to a quick halt. She did a double-take at the tall, thin man who looked so much like Chuck she could hardly believe it wasn't.

He smiled Chuck's smile. Having stopped her car by standing in front of it, he now went around to the passenger's door and calmly opened the door and got in and made himself comfortable on the red-leather bucket seat.

"How do you do," he said. "I'm Chuck's father. I think you're remarkably lovely, if you're Evalin Meeker, and if you're not Evalin Meeker I apologize for this unwarranted invasion."

She swallowed.

"A charming town," said Mr. Jackson. "I'm certain the hotel will be an astonishing success."

Evalin released the brake, shift gears, and the little four-cylinder Morris Minor chugged on again.

"I like your silence," Mr. Jackson said. "Most women talk too much. I deplore that, because when they're talking a man is unable to talk. I looked for you in town."

"What a nice surprise, Mr. Jackson."

"Very professionally said. One can tell by a glance that you run your motel most efficiently and amiably."

She had to laugh.

"Are you in love with my son, Miss Meeker?"

She stopped laughing.

"I hope you are. I know that he is with you. He came to Texas one weekend presumably to discuss business. Actually, most of the talk involved you."

"How could I be? I hardly know him."

Now the car swung into the road leading out of town. Evalin shifted into second and made herself comfortable for the long haul up the winding grade. On their right a gorge appeared, and across the gorge she saw that the shrub-oak was already turning crimson. She inhaled deeply.

"My son, too," said Mr. Jackson, "is concerned because it seemingly lacks logic. You young people are much too logical for your own good."

"Just the same — "

"Well, is he repugnant to you?"

She was so flabbergasted she swung around on her seat. "Golly no! I think he's fine. I think — "

She broke off, blushing.

"How interesting," Mr. Jackson said.

"You have to understand," she said hotly, "that I'm not a giddy fool. All right. I like him very much, and for a lot of reasons that do make sense to me. He could have crushed a ridiculous old man. He didn't. He could have quit when the going was tough. He didn't. He — well, those aren't enough, though. It's a long life together. And I've been foolish once and I don't intend to be foolish again."

"Reasonable."

"You bet it is. And all this means a great deal to me, too. This is home. That's Angel Mountain over there, and all my life I've loved her, and it isn't easy to leave the things you love."

"Except for a deeper, richer love."

"I — "

273

"Well, there's no hurry. We'll be here off and on throughout most of the year ahead. You see, Evalin, I think I approve."

They crested the grade, ran across the little plateau, and Evalin turned the car in between the stone gateposts. She saw Chuck before his cabin, and with him a woman who had to be his mother. She had a sudden strong suspicion that now, his business battle won, Chuck would make her his next project. The suspicion made her heart thump. But she concealed all that, or so she thought, as she acknowledged the introduction to Mrs. Jackson. And she was quite convincingly casual, too, she thought, when Chuck got onto the seat his father had vacated because he'd have to help her unload the groceries. At a snail's pace she drove on up the drive toward the house.

He asked solemnly: "Did you turn Bill down?"

She answered as solemnly: "I turned Bill down."

He nodded. He said huskily: "I love you, Evalin."

She didn't answer. No answer was expected, and anyway it was too early to answer. There'd be weeks and months during which she'd get to know him. They'd ride and they'd ski. They'd go swimming sometimes, and other times they'd go picknicking, and if it was to be it would happen, and if it wasn't to be —

She stopped the car.

Chuck leaned forward. "May I?" he asked.

How strange it was, she thought, nodding, that Andrew was gone and the Wakelys were defeated and Thorpe would progress and yet so many, many things were still the same. There was the motel and there was her home and there were the mountains and the forests. And over all was the vast, beautiful sky of the great beautiful West and —

His lips came down and the kiss stirred her.

He laughed huskily after he'd released her.

"Shall I help you with the groceries?" he asked.

For a moment she couldn't answer. Whatever it was, she was thinking, it was strangely right and good. If it wasn't love, what was it? And if it was love?

Evalin's big blue eyes went round.

She turned and looked at Chuck's face and then, nervous, her nerves tingling, she glanced away.

Good grief, she thought.

"Well?" he asked.

"I think it would be nice," she said.

Impulsively, she leaned forward to kiss him again.

THE END

WITH SOMEBODY ELSE
Theresa Charles

Rosamond sets off for Cornwall with Hugo to meet his family, blissfully unaware of the shocks in store for her.

A SUMMER FOR STRANGERS
Claire Hamilton

Because she had lost her job, her flat and she had no money, Tabitha agreed to pose as Adam's future wife although she believed the scheme to be deceitful and cruel.

VILLA OF SINGING WATER
Angela Petron

The disquieting incidents that occurred at the Vatican and the Colosseum did not trouble Jan at first, but then they became increasingly unpleasant and alarming.

DOCTOR NAPIER'S NURSE
Pauline Ash

When cousins Midge and Derry are entered as probationer nurses on the same day but at different hospitals they agree to exchange identities.

A GIRL LIKE JULIE
Louise Ellis

Caroline absolutely adored Hugh Barrington, but then Julie Crane came into their lives. Julie was the kind of girl who attracts men without even trying.

COUNTRY DOCTOR
Paula Lindsay

When Evan Richmond bought a practice in a remote country village he did not realise that a casual encounter would lead to the loss of his heart.

ENCORE
Helga Moray

Craig and Janet realise that their true happiness lies with each other, but it is only under traumatic circumstances that they can be reunited.

NICOLETTE
Ivy Preston

When Grant Alston came back into her life, Nicolette was faced with a dilemma. Should she follow the path of duty or the path of love?

THE GOLDEN PUMA
Margaret Way

Catherine's time was spent looking after her father's Queensland farm. But what life was there without David, who wasn't interested in her?

HOSPITAL BY THE LAKE
Anne Durham

Nurse Marguerite Ingleby was always ready to become personally involved with her patients, to the despair of Brian Field, the Senior Surgical Registrar, who loved her.

VALLEY OF CONFLICT
David Farrell

Isolated in a hostel in the French Alps, Ann Russell sees her fiancé being seduced by a young girl. Then comes the avalanche that imperils their lives.

NURSE'S CHOICE
Peggy Gaddis

A proposal of marriage from the incredibly handsome and wealthy Reagan was enough to upset any girl — and Brooke Martin was no exception.

A DANGEROUS MAN
Anne Goring

Photographer Polly Burton was on safari in Mombasa when she met enigmatic Leon Hammond. But unpredictability was the name of the game where Leon was concerned.

PRECIOUS INHERITANCE
Joan Moules

Karen's new life working for an authoress took her from Sussex to a foreign airstrip and a kidnapping; to a real life adventure as gripping as any in the books she typed.

VISION OF LOVE
Grace Richmond

When Kathy takes over the rundown country kennels she finds Alec Stinton, a local vet, very helpful. But their friendship arouses bitter jealousy and a tragedy seems inevitable.